ALISON HUNT

Dance a ͏ g

Best wishes
Alison Huntingford x

❋ Lupin Publications ❋

About The Author

Alison Huntingford has a degree in humanities with literature, and has always enjoyed reading, especially, the great writers of the 19th century. She is an only child of two only children and so has always felt a distinct lack of family. This has inspired her to research her family history and most of her writing is based on this. Her debut novel was published in 2019 and was nominated for the Walter Scott Prize for historical fiction. This is her third full length novel, although she has also written several short stories. In her spare time, she enjoys spending time with her husband and their pets, listening to music, going to the cinema, and gardening. She also runs the South Hams Authors Network, a local writers collective based in South Devon. Recently she co-organised two literary festivals.

Other works:

The Glass Bulldog 2019

Someone Else   2020

A Ha'penny Will Do 2022

Editor: Grasping the Nettle, Quirky Tales from the South Hams Authors Network, 2023

A CIP catalogue record for this title is available from the British Library.

ISBN: 978-1-3999-5972-8

Disclaimer

Charles Le Boucher and Rachel Alderman were real people living in Peterborough in the 1800s. Much of this book is based on historical fact, however, whether the two of them actually knew each other is a matter of conjecture and purely the product of the author's overactive imagination! This book is a work of fiction and should be taken as such.

Dedicated to absent friends: my father David and my 'second cousin twice removed', Bill. Much missed.

With love and thanks to my husband Nigel, my godmother Marjorie and all my pets.

'To love or have loved, that is enough. Ask nothing further. There is no other pearl to be found in the dark folds of life.'

Victor Hugo: Les Miserables

Chapter 1

Peterborough 1807

Rachel Alderman had always been considered plain. She was the sort of person who beautiful women smiled at pityingly, whilst silently thanking their lucky stars that they didn't suffer from the same affliction. Her hair was a bit too limp and dark, her face a bit too round, her complexion pale and blotchy. Whilst her figure was pleasing enough, somehow the overall picture just didn't catch the eye. Gentlemen admirers had been thin on the ground over the years, even when she was in her prime. A young sheep farmer had courted her for a while but then turned his attentions to another who had golden ringlets and rosy cheeks. With time Rachel had learned to live with it, waiting patiently for love to arrive, but it seemed to have passed her by. Now, at age 41, she had given it up as a lost cause.

As a child Rachel was shy and quiet. She tended to blush and stammer when having to speak to anyone apart from her family, and as she got older, it got worse. The sixth of seven children, she was yet another mouth to feed, another burden on the family finances and, (it could be said), a bit overlooked. Her parents, Henry and Rebecca Alderman, were warm and caring but they struggled to get by, just to survive. Rachel's problem was something that they didn't have the time to worry about. Trying to keep the family fed was all they could think of. Henry was a lowly paid worker in the local brick making industry; one of the area's main occupations, the other being wool production.

Life in Peterborough in the eighteenth century was hard. By reason of it having a cathedral, it was officially called a city, but was barely much more than a small market town. The streets were merely dirt tracks in places, thick with horse dung and other dubious substances. A trip to the shop could be hazardous to the health, not only from disease, but also from the local rakes who prowled the area hoping to catch out the unwary. Beggars, thieves and harlots lived out their sad lives in the darkness of the back streets whilst poor working families like their own just tried to get by. The only advantage to its location was that it was on the River Nene which had a port navigable to ships, meaning trade flourished. Her father would often tell them how the ships would be taking his bricks far away to strange places they had never heard of.

'Gentlefolk will live in fine houses built with my bricks,' he said proudly, 'and yet we'll never meet. Just fancy that!'

As Rachel grew up, improvements came slowly to the city. There was great excitement among the local population when in 1774 a theatre opened, though the working classes could not, as a rule, afford to go there. It was a period of extravagant manners and elegant balls, which Rachel dreamed of going to, but they were far out of her reach. In her mind's eye she saw herself swirling around the dance floor in a beautiful silk dress.

'But then,' she thought, 'how would I ever face all those people?' and she knew it was just a fantasy. It was well known that a ball was often the only way that single people could talk to each other unchaperoned, and unfortunately, conversation did not come naturally for Rachel.

Of all her family Rachel was closest to her married older sister, Mary, who supported her through a difficult adolescence. Two of their siblings sadly died young, leaving Rachel to dwell on the unfairness of life, and like many another teenager, she sank into melancholy. Black moods came upon her like dark clouds on the horizon and she could not shake them off easily. Mary was a warm and jolly person who always seemed to be able to make Rachel laugh when she was feeling low, which dispelled her gloom. Rachel felt at ease with Mary in a way she rarely did with anyone else. They had always been close despite, or maybe because of, their age difference (twelve years). Mary tended to 'mother' Rachel, which was just what she needed.

Rachel had few friends, not knowing how to talk to people easily and avoiding eye contact wherever possible. It just wasn't comfortable for her. A cold sweat of fear broke out on her brow whenever she had to face anyone. Hence, she got a reputation for being stand-offish and unfriendly, which was in fact very far from the truth. Loneliness and isolation seemed to be her lot, and the lonelier she got, the more she struggled to make friends. At times thoughts of self-destruction ran through her head, but she was sensible enough not to pursue this further. Instead, she often took refuge in Mary's house, helping with her young nieces and nephews. Somehow, she could communicate with the children in a way she never could with people of her own age. There were endless games and fun with no expectations or worries.

As Rachel reached the full adult age of 21, her brother William and his wife Ann tried to get her to meet more eligible young men. A gentle dalliance began hesitantly with Tommy, a sheep farmer's son. Rachel had been shyly admiring him for many months before she finally admitted it to her sister-in-law. Ann wasted no time in making contact with the lad, ensuring that some excuse was found for him to visit the family home. He was reluctant, but Ann persuaded him it could be worth his while and to start with things seemed to go well. After a few hesitant meetings, however, disaster struck.

Mary, who was now in her thirties and pregnant for the fifth time, became very ill. Rachel spent hours looking after her prior to the impending birth but was filled with dread. Childbirth was a risky business, she knew.

'I'll be alright,' insisted Mary cheerfully. 'You don't need to worry.'

'Of course you will,' replied Rachel. 'As soon as the baby's born, you'll be up and about in no time.'

But Mary's face was flushed and feverish, and secretly everyone was anxious about her.

A couple of days later Rachel awoke, after a disturbing dream, with a feeling of foreboding. The dawn was just appearing in the sky, but it was full of angry storm clouds, tinged blood red at the edges. The wind was howling mournfully around their cottage. Her mother's anxious call had been what roused her. Mary was in labour and needed her sister. Rachel rushed to be by her side.

Hours of pain and exhaustion wore on, Mary becoming weaker and weaker, until at last the baby was delivered. Sadly, despite the best efforts of the midwife, the baby was born dead, the result of a prolonged and difficult labour. Mary cried out weakly:

'My baby – please give him to me – let me hold him!'

Then as the weather raged overhead, she collapsed and died.

Rachel wept for days, not knowing how she would ever get over the loss of her beloved sister, who had always been such a comfort to her. Sometimes in the early hours she would lie awake, thinking it all over and remembering, until she made herself cry all over again. Death was so final, she realised. There were no more chances to talk to the loved one; to hug them, to laugh with them, even to argue with them. It was all gone.

For the moment, however, practicalities had to be attended to. Mary's husband, John Baker, needed help looking after their children and everyone seemed to think that Rachel was the best candidate for the job. Her other siblings were all married now, and she was, after all, very fond of the infants.

Rachel saw Tommy in the street shortly after the funeral and had to tell him that she was now fully occupied and unable to see him for the time being.

'But what about us?' he asked, angry and hurt.

'I'm sorry,' she explained, 'I need to help my family. It won't be forever. Maybe in the future we could…'

'I can't wait around for you!' he declared. 'I've a life to live. There are other far prettier girls around here only too happy to be taken out by me. I was just being kind anyway. You'll turn into an old maid, and you'll only have yourself to blame!'

His bitter words stung her deep inside and she turned away in tears. What could she say?

So it was that any possible romantic liaisons were stifled, and Rachel became housekeeper and surrogate mother to four children, all aged under 6. Sarah was the eldest, then James aged 4, Mary Ann aged 3 and baby Edward. Rachel moved into the cottage, sleeping in a spare bed in the same room as her charges. They were sweet natured, well-behaved children who already knew their aunt well, so they adapted quickly to the loss of their mother. Their father, John, worked hard from early until late and they saw little of him, except at supper time. He was grateful for Rachel's help, but seemingly unaware that her life was on hold.

The first anniversary of Mary's death came around and Rachel couldn't help thinking about it, try as she might. However, she distracted herself (and the children, who were blissfully unaware) by keeping busy. They went on a long walk down by the river in Peterborough, finding and collecting wildflowers. She'd mostly succeeded in putting it from her mind until after the children had gone to bed and she was sat down doing the darning. Her brother-in-law John had seemed quiet and morose at supper, and he was sunk in thought now. Suddenly he declared:

'I still miss her, you know!'

'Mary?' said Rachel.

'Yes, she's still so much in my mind. You know it's a year today, don't you?'

Rachel nodded.

'I can feel her all around me, everywhere I go, and yet she's not here. It's not fair!', he exclaimed bitterly. Then he softened.

'I'm sorry. You must miss her too. Look at you - taking care of us all as usual. What would we do without you?'

His voice trembled and his hands shook with emotion.

Rachel reached forward and patted his hand, feeling suddenly close to him. There was an awkward silence for a moment, then John stood up. He sounded embarrassed.

'I'm going to the alehouse,' he said. 'I won't be late.'

He put on his coat and went out into the night, and the brief intimacy between them vanished like smoke in the breeze.

Nine years passed – nine years in which Rachel did her best to bring up the children. She saw them through scraped knees and childish tantrums, tears and temperatures. She saw the falling out of friendships and the pangs of first love as they grew towards adulthood. Despite having no schooling herself (girls didn't get any lessons back then and boys only rarely), she tried hard to impart what knowledge she had. They learned about the world around them, about nature and the stars, about numbers and the names of things, about cooking and money. In all ways she was like a mother to them; at the same time sharing her memories of their real mother so that they would 'know' Mary, even though she was no longer there. Edward couldn't remember his mother at all, which Rachel found desperately sad. She did her best to fill the void and became very close to the little boy.

In the back of her mind, Rachel harboured the idea that one day, Mary's widowed husband might marry her, at least for the sake of the children. Not that she loved John – she was fond of him and life there felt familiar and comfortable - but romantic love was never an option.

It was a shock therefore when he came home one day in 1796 and told them he was getting married again. It was at the supper table when he suddenly announced it.

'I've got something wonderful to tell you all,' he said, his eyes shining. 'Miss James, from the grocer's shop, has agreed to be my wife!'

There was a stunned silence, then Sarah, the eldest girl, asked:

'Will she come and live here?'

'Yes, of course,' replied John. 'She will be your new mother.'

'But I don't want a new mother!' cried Edward. 'We've got Aunty Rachel. We don't need anyone else.'

Rachel sat there not knowing what to do or say.

'Aunty Rachel will be able to get on with her own life now,' John told his son. 'It's high time she was free of us all.'

Hot tears stung Rachel's eyes and she struggled to contain them. She was so fond of the family and now it seemed like she was being dismissed. More cheerfully than she felt, she managed:

'I think it's very good news. Congratulations! Children, you must wish your father well. It's only right.'

A strained and awkward celebration ensued; not many of them had the heart for it. Alone in her bed that night, Rachel finally let the river of emotions flow. What next for her? She couldn't begin to imagine.

Days passed and they all started to get used to the idea. John brought Miss James home to tea and, in spite of themselves, they all liked her. Ellen was a sweet natured woman in her early twenties, with a soft face and light brown curls. Rachel compared the young woman with herself and realised that she had turned into an old maid, just like Tommy said she would. In the reflection of a shop window, she saw a plain, tired looking woman, just over 30 and probably past all prospects of marriage. Most women married young, and if not, it was likely they would stay single and work for the rest of their lives. Rachel guessed that this was now to be her fate. The charms of youth had slipped away whilst she wasn't looking. She didn't regret looking after the family all these years, but now she had to find something new.

There were very few options for poor, working women then – either domestic service or prostitution; and Rachel did not have the heart, the inclination or the looks for the latter. Domestic service it would have to be, therefore. The obvious thing to do, with all her experience, was to get a job looking after children. Unfortunately, Rachel had no references and could not write, therefore the only way of approaching prospective employers was in person, on foot. For a person of crippling shyness, however, this was no easy feat. All of a sudden, all Rachel's insecurities came flooding back. How could she approach people for employment when she went to pieces talking to anyone new? The last few years had been comfortable for her, only having to deal with her immediate circle and a few local traders. Nevertheless, she knew she must try and overcome her fears this time.

After gaining some local information from her sister-in-law, Ann, Rachel dressed in her best outfit and went to call on some of the larger houses in Peterborough. At the first one, she was dismayed to find that the haughty butler turned her away before she barely got started. As he opened the door, she felt herself going red and without meaning to, she wrung her hands anxiously. She could hardly speak for nervousness. He sneered at her and shut the door firmly.

Over the next couple of weeks this was an occurrence that was often to be repeated. Others had no work available. Worse still was the occasion when she was laughed at and rejected rudely whilst trying to explain the reason for her visit.

'Clear off!' cried the woman who opened the door. 'We ain't taking no charity cases 'ere!'

After several long fruitless days, Rachel finally called at the local parsonage. Her hopes were low, knowing how little rectors earned, despite their genteel appearances. She knocked gingerly, almost frightened to make yet another attempt. This time however a kindly looking woman, (the housekeeper, Rachel guessed, from the bunch of keys hanging at her waist), came to the door.

'I, er…' Rachel stammered, going crimson, 'I wondered if there was any work here. I mean, that is, if you want anyone, well that is….' Her voice trailed off. Her face was flushed, and she realised what a mess she was making of this. She could feel the tears coming into her eyes. To her surprise the woman smiled.

'You after a job, are you, dearie? What sort of thing?'

Rachel relaxed a bit.

'I'm very good with children,' she replied eagerly, 'and I can cook.'

The woman shook her head.

'Sorry dearie, we already got a nursemaid. All we got going is a house maid post. It's hard work, long hours and you'll have to sleep in the basement, but you could do worse. The Rector and his missus are decent, though they don't pay too well. There's only a few of us here so we all have to pitch in together.'

Rachel's heart sank but she didn't have many options. The housekeeper offered her a week's trial and she took it.

John and Ellen's wedding took place the following week and Rachel had to admit to herself that she felt quite jealous. Ellen looked lovely in a simple white muslin dress, complete with demure lace cap, as was the fashion in those days. Rachel wondered if she would ever get her chance to walk down the aisle but knew this was unlikely. A spinster she was, and a spinster she would probably stay. Later, she told herself firmly that marriage and children were not the 'be all and end all'. There was life outside of that, but whether she believed this was another matter.

Saying goodbye to the children was hard. Sarah, now 16 years old, bravely tried to wish her well but everyone else was too choked up to do more than hug her fondly. Rachel could hardly speak for emotion but finally wrenched herself away from their clinging embraces, picked up her bags and walked out the door. Young Edward ran after her, crying, but she didn't dare turn around otherwise she might never have left. She went straight to the vicarage.

Chapter 2

Mrs Briggs, the housekeeper, was a kindly soul and did her best to make Rachel feel at home. Firstly, she was introduced to the only upstairs servant; the somewhat snooty and condescending nanny/governess, Jane. They observed polite formalities, but it was clear that the children's nurse was uninterested in the new arrival. Rachel asked after the children enthusiastically and was told that Jane's main task was to make sure that they didn't bother the master and mistress.

'But surely,' Rachel asked awkwardly, 'they want to see their children?'

'When they're older, maybe,' replied Jane, 'but everyone knows children aren't worth bothering with at this age.'

Rachel reflected on this silently and knew it was current thinking amongst gentlefolk, but she couldn't understand it herself. Children could give such pleasure. Their parents didn't know what they were missing.

'Well at least you have the joy of them,' she said to Jane, 'and can love them.'

'Love them?' said Jane scornfully. 'I'm here to teach and discipline them, not to bother with that stuff.'

Rachel turned bright red, realising how outspoken she had been, unlike her normal self. It was just that she felt so strongly about it, but she said no more. It wasn't her place to argue.

Next, Mrs Briggs gave her a tour around the house and garden. As they were progressing up the stairs to the first floor, they came across the gentleman of the house, Reverend Forster, and immediately made way for him to pass. It wasn't done to intrude upon a master's space in general, but on this occasion, he stopped, noticing a new face.

'Hello, Mrs Briggs,' he said pleasantly, 'and who do we have here?'

'This is the new housemaid, Sir. She starts today.'

'Rachel Alderman at your service, Sir,' Rachel murmured timidly and curtseyed.

The rector was dressed all in black with an old-fashioned powdered wig which moved around as he spoke.

'You're very welcome, my dear,' he said. 'Rachel – that's a good biblical name. I hope your family observe all the religious rites and go to church on Sundays and holy days.'

'Oh yes, Sir,' she replied, blushing with embarrassment at being spoken to by a gentleman. 'They have always been churchgoers.'

Whilst strictly speaking this was true, Rachel had to admit to herself that her family only went because it was the custom, not because of any deeply held beliefs.

The Reverend smiled, pleased with her answer.

'God be with you, my child,' he said and passed on down the stairs. This was to be the only time he spoke to Rachel in all her time at the vicarage. As was normal at that time, masters and servants didn't mix and rarely communicated.

Out in the garden Mrs Briggs showed Rachel the fruit and

vegetable plot where the cook would gather what materials she needed for dinner each day.

'James looks after the garden,' Mrs Briggs told Rachel, 'And the horses. He sees to the wood for the fires as well and does any other heavy work required. You'll usually find him out in the stables if you need him; he sleeps there. Don't know what we'd do without him.'

Rachel's attention was suddenly caught by a tree at the end of the garden. The dark trunk and bare branches stood out against the winter sky, and to her horror Rachel noticed a rope hanging down from one of the branches, which instantly made her think of a gallows pole. She had passed the public gallows in Peterborough often enough, but always took care not to be around when a public hanging was due. She'd also sheltered Mary's children from such scenes. The whole thought made her shudder and yet held a terrible fascination for her.

'What's that?' she asked the housekeeper nervously.

'Oh, just a rope that the local children like to play on. The master doesn't like it much, but it's hard to stop them. After all, they haven't got anywhere else to go.'

Rachel breathed a sigh of relief and felt embarrassed for thinking such a thing.

After meeting the rest of the servants – Betty the cook and the young scullery maid, Annie; Rachel was shown where she would be sleeping. She was shocked and a little dismayed to find her bed would be just a thin mattress on the floor, along with the others. Still, she was determined to make the best of it. It was a job and a home of sorts and was the most she could hope for at present.

Time passed and Rachel settled into the routine of her new life.

The week's trial proved satisfactory, and her position was made permanent, which at least was reassuring. The working day was long and hard, but she didn't complain. Her role included cleaning grates, lighting fires, dusting and general cleaning, emptying chamber pots, trimming and lighting candles and much more besides. With such a small staff they had often had to pull together to help in other areas as well. Not that the vicar and his wife were given to entertaining. They lived simply without a great deal of fuss, but to a certain standard all the same.

At first Rachel felt shy with the other staff, especially whilst sharing their cramped, basic living quarters. However, the demanding daily routine left little time for anything except essential communication, for which she was grateful. She kept herself to herself, barely having time to think, let alone chat. This suited her in one way, but in another she felt dreadfully lonely. At least she had had human contact whilst looking after Mary's children. Now, there was almost none, despite being surrounded by people. Mrs Briggs was a cheerful woman but was always busy. Annie the scullery maid was a cheeky young thing, always chasing after the local delivery boys, and frequently scolded by Betty, the stern and rather sour faced cook. James was an older man, only interested in his horses; and Jane, they rarely saw. So, all in all, it was a lonely job and Rachel grew ever more inward looking.

Occasionally Rachel passed the Rector's two sons, sailing along like small silent ships in the wake of their governess. But there was no joy in their faces and Rachel felt sorry for them. She remembered all the happiness she'd had with her nieces and nephews, hunting for berries in the garden, gathering flowers by the river, baking bread or lighting fires. It had all been a great game for them, a new adventure every day. She realised now that this had been the happiest time of her life so far.

On her rare days off she tried to keep in touch with her sister's family. Rachel's natural reticence however, prevented her from visiting them at their home. She felt that she shouldn't intrude upon Ellen's domain. After all it was her household now. Sadly, this meant she saw less of the children than she would have liked. Nevertheless, she did manage one joyful day with Sarah, now going on 17 and properly in love for the first time. They met up in town and spent their time browsing the shops for hats and trimmings. The shop assistants were only too keen to help the attractive young lady with Rachel, but not so enthusiastic in dealing with her. When she enquired about a new hat in one shop, the assistant remarked haughtily:

'Begging your pardon, Ma'am, but that's more for younger folks. A more matronly style like these would suit you.'

She produced one of the ugliest hats that Rachel had ever seen and proceeded to extol its virtues for a 'lady of her age'. Rachel's cheeks burned like fire as she attempted feebly to explain that she didn't like it, and she was only saved from making an unwanted purchase by Sarah who interjected:

'Oh no, that's dreadful. We certainly don't want that!'

Rachel wished she could have been so outspoken and honest, but it just wasn't her nature. As they retreated hastily, Rachel caught sight of herself in the shop mirror and had to admit that she looked like an old matron. Fashions were changing to a simpler, more streamlined, dress style, but she still wore an old fashioned full skirted dark brocade dress, with layers of lace around her bodice preserving her modesty. Her large round face was lined with wrinkles now and her hair was scraped back in a severe bun. No matter what she did with it, it never seemed to look right, so this seemed the best option. She was not aware that this made her look stern and unapproachable.

Sarah, however (who of all the children was most like her dear Mary), cheered her up with a gentle stream of pleasant, youthful banter and the day was passed most agreeably after all.

Sometimes in the kitchen Rachel couldn't help overhearing the local gossip. Annie was always recounting tasty titbits that she'd gleaned from her latest flame – the butcher's boy or the baker's lad – which kept them entertained in the kitchen. It was the spring of 1797 when Annie declared the town was being 'simply invaded by them Frenchies.'

'Them's everywhere,' she told them, 'Out and about. T'aint right.'

'What on earth are you on about, girl?' demanded Betty, sharply.

'They'm all coming from the prison camp. You know, the new one up at Norman Cross. Opened in April. They say they're all Napoleon's soldiers.'

Mrs Briggs came in at that point and confirmed what Annie had said. A prisoner of war camp had been built to house the French soldiers captured in the Napoleonic wars. It was the first of its kind and supposed to be a model of moderation. Many of the soldiers (though mostly officers) were allowed a certain amount of liberty and were able to mingle with the townspeople at times.

'T'aint right,' repeated Annie. 'Dirty Frenchies out and about everywhere. We might all get murdered in our beds!'

Mrs Briggs sought to calm her fears.

'I don't think that's likely, Annie. They're soldiers, not criminals. They've just had the misfortune to be captured that's all. Folks say the camp treats them well in the hope that the French will do the same for our boys.'

'Humph!' snorted Betty. 'Fat chance of that!'

'Well, that's the theory,' Mrs Briggs replied.

Rachel didn't take much notice of the conversation at the time, but on her next monthly day off, whilst going to visit her family, she was shocked to notice how busy the town was. Soldiers in ragged uniforms with strange accents wandered amongst the local population. The marketplace was heaving with hawkers trying to sell hand-made goods and Rachel was accosted more than once on her way to her parent's home. Peterborough was bustling.

There was a certain amount of resentment in the neighbourhood, but it was undeniable that the city was flourishing because of the new arrivals. So many more services and provisions were needed, and the local tradesmen were happy to supply them. Over the next few years, the city would grow rapidly.

Her parents though had other views.

'There's too many of 'em,' said her mother. 'They're everywhere, eating our food and taking over the market. Your father's worried about whether he'll get his job back once he's better.'

Henry Alderman was now frail and infirm, and Rachel was sad to see it. Secretly she doubted whether he would ever be well enough to work again. A lifetime of hard labour in the brick industry had taken its toll, and the dust had affected his lungs, so much so that he could no longer do his job. Every breath was an enormous effort. His grown-up children, Rachel included, all contributed towards their parents' upkeep, otherwise it would have been the poorhouse for them. These were no times for those who couldn't earn a living. Rachel felt glad that at least she had her health.

She couldn't share her parents' views about the prison camp, however. Privately, she found herself pitying the prisoners. After all, they were far from home, cut off from their loved ones and deprived of their freedom, even if they were being treated well. It couldn't be easy.

Months went by and the small city got used to the influx of people and what's more, began to prosper. There were even enough funds for the local authorities to begin a large scale clean up and improvement to the local streets, paving them and adding street lighting; making Peterborough a safer and healthier place to live. The population of the area had more than doubled but it was certainly a benefit rather than a disadvantage. Years of the King's uncertain health combined with a costly series of overseas wars meant that the country as a whole was struggling, but their city seemed to be defying the odds. French officers and their wives could often be seen promenading around and it was rumoured that, rather than being made to live in the prison camp, they actually had fine houses in the town. Some even said that the prisoners were taking local women as mistresses. Even the vicarage seemed to get increasingly busy with visitors and Rachel was shocked to hear French accents from some whilst taking up the afternoon tea one day. When she mentioned it to the others Mrs Briggs smiled slightly and said knowingly:

'Well, that's where all the money is, these days, m'dear. Can't blame the Rector for trying to get his share, I guess.'

Things had certainly changed in Peterborough.

Chapter 3

The eighteenth century was waning like the moon in the sky, and everyone was waiting for the new one to arise. Three years had gone by at the vicarage, and in that time, there had been some changes.

Annie had finally taken a step too far with the baker's boy and got herself 'in the family way'. She retreated to her mother's house where, it was said, she'd had a baby girl following a very hasty wedding. Needless to say, they saw no more of her at the vicarage and a replacement – little Emily – was found. Emily was an orphan (of about 12 years old it was guessed) and as innocent as a newly hatched chick. Much to everyone's surprise, sour old Betty took her under her wing and coaxed her along through her duties.

Mrs Briggs had been ill with the influenza on one occasion, and a sprained ankle on another and Rachel was called upon to deputise for her both times.

'But I can't!' she protested the first time she was asked. 'I don't know how.'

'You know almost as much as I do,' replied the housekeeper from her bed, 'and you're very capable and reliable. You'll be fine, I'm sure.'

In spite of Rachel's self-doubt, she found herself rising to the challenge and, what's more, enjoying it.

Yes, she thought, it wasn't really so different from running the household when she had charge of her nephews and nieces. Maybe she could do it. Perhaps this might be an idea for the future?

Her confidence was unexpectedly boosted by the experience.

Jane, the governess, got a shock when the Rector and his wife decided to send their two sons away to boarding school, and promptly dispensed with her services. Rachel felt a bit sorry for her at first, but then she remembered Jane's hard-hearted attitude to the children and thought better of it.

Sadly, Rachel's father finally succumbed to a lifetime of brick dust the previous year and Rachel still mourned him now. Her mother moved in with her married sister Elizabeth White and things went back to some semblance of normality, but her family would never be the same again. Mrs Briggs had kindly given Rachel a day off to attend the funeral, a favour that was rarely given when 'in service', and which she much appreciated.

As the century slowly sickened and died, Rachel too felt her own health decay. At first, she thought it was just her age, after all she was 35 now and people rarely lived past 50 in those days. Her hands, which after several years of manual toil were hard and calloused, had suddenly become sore with lesions which bled regularly. She guessed it was just a new dish soap that they were using, but they hurt a lot. Then blisters also appeared further up her arms and she began to get a bit worried. Not one to make a fuss, she carried on, denying to herself just how ill she was feeling. Some mornings now she could hardly drag herself from her mattress on the floor, for the dizziness, tiredness and pain she felt.

'You look peaky,' said Betty, in her usual forthright manner.

'Need to get some good food inside yer. Here, take a dish of this.'

She handed Rachel a large plate of stew, but after taking a few mouthfuls she felt quite sick. Making her excuses she rushed outside to get some air. In her heart Rachel knew something was wrong, but she couldn't afford to stop work. She had to earn a living.

Things finally came to a head one day in the early autumn of 1800 when Rachel was in the kitchen collecting the afternoon tea. The room seemed to be spinning around, and she broke out into a cold sweat. She tried to speak but her voice failed. Then she passed out into blackness, collapsing on the floor with a clatter of broken teacups.

Rachel came to in a soft bed, gazing up at her sister Elizabeth and a man she'd never seen before, who turned out to be the doctor. She felt dreadful and could hardly speak for weakness.

'Lie still,' the doctor ordered. 'You must rest. You're not at all well. I've given you something to help you sleep.'

Rachel sank into darkness once again, this time allowing it to swallow her up in its warm depths. It was some time before she surfaced again. When she awoke the pale autumn sunlight was pouring through the window into the room and Elizabeth sat there smiling. Rachel struggled to sit up, but her sister stopped her gently.

'You must take it easy, Rachel. You're still very weak. Let me fetch you some broth, it'll do you good.'

Rachel tried a few mouthfuls, but it made her feel sick.

'What's wrong with me?' she croaked. 'How long have I been here?'

'The doctor says you have had arsenic poisoning,' Elizabeth explained. 'You nearly died, but you're just about out of danger now.'

'Arsenic! How? It can't be!' spluttered Rachel. (Everyone had heard of the lethal substance).

'Easy there,' Elizabeth said, 'The doctor said it was probably from some household product that you've been using – maybe rat poison or candles. Some of the cheap ones are mixed with arsenic to save money.'

'The tallow ones?' Rachel asked weakly and Elizabeth nodded.

Rachel groaned. 'We use those all the time at the vicarage. If only I'd known.'

'The doctor says it is a very slow process in these cases; little by little it grows in you and makes you ill.'

'I must get back to work! I must tell them. How did I get here?'

Then Elizabeth recounted how Mrs Briggs had contacted them, and with James' help she'd been brought over by horse and cart, for Elizabeth and their mother to nurse. They had taken turns in sitting with her throughout. The doctor had been a regular visitor.

'But the doctor's fees,' said Rachel, panicking. 'I must pay you!'

'There's no need to worry. Your employer, Reverend Forster has paid them. When the doctor told him what had happened, he felt responsible and sent him the money immediately.'

'He's a good man,' sighed Rachel and fell back on her pillow, exhausted.

During those first days of illness Rachel implored her sister to bring someone to her so that she could make her will. She had no knowledge whether she would ever recover her health, and although she possessed little of value, she wanted to make sure her affairs were in order. Thinking it through in her sick bed, Rachel decided to leave everything equally divided between her brothers, her sister Elizabeth and her children, and dear Mary's children. They were, after all, the ones she loved the best and who had loved her in return. At least they would benefit when the time came for her goods to be disposed of. She was so insistent that Elizabeth gave in and dutifully found two local notaries to come and assist Rachel in making her testament. It took some days because Rachel was so ill that she could not converse for long. Despite this she managed to compose the following:

'I Rachel Alderman of Peterboro' in the county of Northampton, spinster, being sick and weak in body but of sound mind and memory …. do make publish and declare this to be my last Will and Testament……'

Unfortunately, Rachel had never been taught to write and so could not sign her own name, but she made her mark in front of witnesses and so it was done at last. Now she could relax. Whatever became of her now did not matter, she thought. Her wishes had been made clear; and her nearest and dearest would know how much she had cared about them when her time on earth was done.

One day Sarah and Edward came to visit Rachel, but she was still so weak that she couldn't see them for very long, which made her feel sad.

'Don't worry, Aunty Rachel, we'll come back very soon,' promised Edward and left a bunch of flowers he had brought for her. The sight of them cheered Rachel each time she awoke and made her resolve to get strong again.

Doctor Baxter smiled the next time he saw Rachel. She was propped up in bed, trying her best to eat soup.

'That's good,' he said encouragingly. 'You must eat to get your strength back. The arsenic has passed out of your system now, but the effects will last for a fair while yet, I'm afraid, maybe weeks. You've been very lucky to survive. A poor man I saw a couple of weeks ago in the same plight wasn't so fortunate. His funeral is tomorrow.' Rachel shivered at the thought.

After the doctor had gone Rachel was left deep in thought. Elizabeth had been with her and as she left the room she said:

'Well, that's wonderful, isn't it? You've got another chance at life. How many people get that? Make sure you don't waste it!'

The words were spoken cheerfully and with good intent, but they sank deep into Rachel's consciousness. In her mind she reviewed her life so far. What had she done? She hadn't married or had a family. She hadn't even been in love to speak of. Her virtue was still intact, and she had never experienced passion. Her life had been one of missed chances. Her shyness had been like a prison inside, holding her back. Oh, how she wished it could have been different. Even her choice of job had been forced upon her by circumstance. Tears of self-pity threatened to engulf her. Her life was a waste, she thought, she had done so little and missed out on so much. How could she have let that happen?

Her mind whirled with regret. She had never travelled, never been to a ball. Her choice of clothes, hairstyle and home had all been severely limited. She was embarrassed to admit that she was aware that she looked dowdy, old fashioned and plain. Only the other day she'd overheard the local delivery lad laughing with his mates as he went down the lane, having delivered his wares at the vicarage.

'What an ugly old hag!' he'd exclaimed.

'Who? The housekeeper?' his friend asked.

'No, that old maid, the one who does the cleaning. Crikey – who'd be seen with her? Looks like a horse!'

They went off shrieking with laughter, but Rachel had heard every word. They were right of course, she admitted now. She'd let herself go, but how could that have been helped?

Gloom descended on Rachel like the fog rolling in from the sea, and depression overcame her. Next time Elizabeth came in she found her in floods of bitter tears.

'What have I done?' Rachel cried plaintively. 'I've wasted my life! Now it's all too late and I haven't done anything.'

Her sister did her best to comfort and soothe her, begging her to rest and be calm.

'You need to recover,' she told her. 'You won't if you carry on like this. There's all the time in the world to change things if you want to, but you have to get well first. Now please take this and get some sleep.'

Then Elizabeth administered a sedative that the doctor had prescribed in case of distress, and Rachel slept at last.

The following days were full of tears and bitter regret. At times Rachel raged against the vagaries of life, at other times she raged against herself. There seemed no end to her despair. Poor Elizabeth's patience was sorely tried.

Next time the doctor visited he found Rachel in very low spirits, despite slowly improving in health.

'Now come on, Miss,' he admonished sternly, 'You need to cheer up and get well. All this crying will wear you out.'

'I want to get back to work,' she said tearfully. 'I need to be useful again.'

'Well, it can't be rushed, you know,' he replied. 'What's more when you do go back to work it needs to be lighter duties. You're not as strong as you used to be, so maybe you should consider doing a different job.'

This did nothing to help raise Rachel's low mood. How could she earn a living in any other way? What could she do?

Next day she was saved from further pondering by a visit from Mrs Briggs. The kind and cheery housekeeper was relieved to see Rachel beginning to recover.

'My dear girl, I'm glad to see you're looking better. We were all very worried about you. I told the Reverend those cheap candles were no good. Just a skinflint, he is! Anyway, they're all gone now.'

They chatted generally for a while but then Rachel was dismayed to hear that they'd found another girl to take her place.

'Had to,' said Mrs Briggs apologetically. 'The Master and Missus have got to have their staff. The Missus had a dinner party arranged, so she insisted we take on someone else to help. Anyway, you're in no fit state to work yet, let's face it.'

'Can I come back again later' asked Rachel, 'when I'm well?'

Mrs Briggs looked a bit embarrassed.

'Well,' she said awkwardly, 'of course, if there's a vacancy, but it wouldn't be fair to kick the other girl out now, would it? I'd be happy to give you an excellent reference. Maybe you could think about progressing.'

'What do you mean?' asked Rachel.

'Well, up to a housekeeper's job like mine. I mean you're very capable and it's not such hard manual work, which might be better for you.'

Rachel thought for a moment. 'The doctor did say I had to take it a bit easier now. But I'm no good at approaching people. I'll never be able to do it. I'm too shy, you see.'

Mrs Briggs patted her hand.

'I'm sure you can do it, dear. You get on fine with all of us after all.'

'But I know you!' protested Rachel. 'It's different.'

'Well just pretend you know these other people,' Mrs Briggs suggested. 'Look, I've got an idea. When you're well enough to work, I'll help you make contacts with employers to find you a housekeeping position. I know lots of people in Peterborough.'

'Would you really help me?' asked Rachel, looking happier.

'Certainly. You're a really good worker and we're all very fond of you.'

'Really?' said Rachel, surprised, 'but I thought no-one even knew me.'

Mrs Briggs smiled. 'Of course we do,' she said. 'After all, when you work and live as closely as we all have for the last three years, it's impossible not to know someone!'

It suddenly occurred to Rachel that this was true. They'd become part of each other's lives and yet she'd never realised it. She would be sorry to leave and move on, but it seemed that fate had intervened again.

There was a lot to consider when Mrs Briggs left, and Rachel started to feel a bit more positive. Later that afternoon, this was further compounded by her mother coming in to give her a pep talk.

'Look Rachel,' said her mother (never one to waste her words), 'it's time you pulled yourself together. Poor Elizabeth has been waiting on you hand and foot, and all you've been doing is moaning and crying. It's not fair, you know. We all know you've been ill, but it's time you made an effort.'

In her heart, Rachel knew her mother was right and resolved to change her attitude. Her poor sister!

'I know, Mother,' she said, 'and I'm sorry. I really will try to be better, and I'm going to start right now. Can you help me into that chair, please? It's time I got out of bed.'

So, Rachel came to the decision that she would transform her life. It was not too late, she told herself. It could be done. She knew she would need help, but after all, what were families for? She just wasn't sure where to start.

Chapter 4

Over the next few weeks there was a steady trickle of visitors who all helped to cheer up and encourage Rachel. Mary's four children, now all teenagers, came to visit and she also got to know Elizabeth's family a lot better. There were three healthy sons, all growing up fast, like shoots in a cornfield. Elizabeth was delighted to see her sister improving in health and in spirits. Rachel was now up and about, though still not very strong. She tired easily.

One day the two sisters had a heart-to-heart talk. It was a cold winter's afternoon, and a few flakes of snow were gently falling, soft in the icy air. They were sat by the fireside quite alone. Everyone else had gone out. It was a rare moment of tranquillity.

'Elizabeth,' Rachel began hesitantly, 'I'm sorry I gave you such a hard time whilst I was ill.'

'Forget it!' replied Elizabeth cheerfully. 'What are sisters for?'

'I wanted to ask you something,' continued Rachel, 'well, it's a bit awkward really.'

'Anything,' said Elizabeth, 'just name it.'

'Well, I want to change myself.'

'Change? How? In what way?'

'In every way,' Rachel told her in a decided tone. 'My looks, my job, my home and most of all, me – my shyness I mean. It is so hard to talk to people and it holds me back. If only I could talk to strangers like I can to you.'

'All I can suggest,' said Elizabeth thoughtfully, 'is that you relax more and don't try so hard. We're all strangers to start with, after all. You're fine when you get to know people. Maybe you should just try and imagine you've met them already? We're all the same underneath, you know.'

Realising that this was true, Rachel smiled. She felt better already.

Rachel tried, she really tried, but transformation is not as easy as it sounds. Unfortunately, instant makeovers only happen in fairy stories, not real life, and reforming a lifetime's habits and behaviour is no mean feat. In the end she reasoned that little by little was best and most likely to succeed.

Starting off was exciting and fun. With Sarah and Elizabeth's help she changed her hairstyle and clothes to make herself appear softer and more approachable. Out went the dark, frumpy, heavy brocade frocks to be replaced by simpler, lighter, more streamlined dresses which made her feel as if she was floating on air. Not that there was money available for a whole new wardrobe, but between them they managed to make over several old dresses belonging to her sister in laws, Ellen and Ann, who were quite similar in build to Rachel. A ribbon here, a touch of lace there, freshened up the tired old clothes and made them smile again. Then Sarah showed her how to dress her hair more becomingly and a dainty lace cap set it all off. When Rachel saw herself in the looking glass, she could hardly believe her eyes.

As for Rachel's inner changes, however, she still felt as if she was held captive behind the bars of her insecurities. Every time she struggled to break free, she ended up in the same cell again. Remembering what Mrs Briggs had promised she resolved to contact her with a view to getting started on her job search, but days came, and days went and still she hadn't got round to it. There never seemed to be the time, she told herself, but she knew deep down that she was making excuses. She'd always found it difficult asking people for favours, even after they'd been offered. It just didn't come naturally to her.

Now she was well again she spent time helping out around the house and looking after Elizabeth's three children, but she knew this couldn't carry on forever. She was a financial burden that the family couldn't afford to have. The time was fast approaching when she must leave.

Thankfully Mrs Briggs ended the stalemate by paying another visit, this time with some news for Rachel.

'I've made contact with several of my colleagues around town,' she told her. 'There's a sort of housekeeper's network and we all know each other. Anyway, there's a couple of positions going shortly, that would suit you down to the ground. I've brought pen and paper so let's write some letters today.'

'Today?' stammered Rachel, flustered. 'But I can't!'

'You can and you will,' said Mrs Briggs firmly but kindly. 'You can tell me what to put and I'll write the letters for you.'

Two hours later Rachel had to agree that it had been a useful afternoon's work. Mrs Briggs was wonderful at coaxing the details of Rachel's experience out of her and putting it all down, so that it sounded impressive.

'Have I really done all that?' said Rachel when Mrs Briggs read it back to her.

'Yes indeed,' she answered, 'and more besides, probably. It's amazing what skills life gives us.'

'You're a good friend,' Rachel said impulsively, 'and I'm very grateful, Mrs Briggs.'

'Please call me Rose, my dear. We're friends after all. And you don't need to thank me, you're very welcome.'

Three weeks later Rachel was standing in the parlour of a member of the Peterborough clergy, giving an account of her experience, so that they could decide on her suitability for the post. Reverend Tutte was a middle-aged gentleman with grey hair and whiskers, who lived with his recently widowed younger sister, Mrs Green, a lady of refined sensibilities and delicate health. Dressed all in black with a lace veil, she looked as if she might blow away at the slightest breath of wind. The Reverend was a serious man, much given to wandering around the house at all hours, rehearsing his sermons out loud. (The maid warned Rachel about this, telling her just to ignore him and not be frightened if she came upon him in the middle of the night). He was based at Peterborough Cathedral and earned a good living due to his status.

They asked Rachel a few questions which she answered confidently, having been well rehearsed by Mrs Briggs and Elizabeth beforehand. The interview went well, and Rachel was offered the post. She was to start the following week and would be required to take charge of the household and the other two servants. There was a small staff, just the cook and a general maid. The house was a well-appointed town house on the outskirts of the cathedral grounds and Rachel was pleased to find that she would have her own bedroom and a small housekeeper's office. What luxury, she thought, a real step up in the world.

After touring round the servant's quarters on her first day, she made up her mind to upgrade them. She wasn't having her staff sleeping on the floor. She knew what that was like. There was room in the basement for two small beds and she set about arranging it immediately. The Reverend frowned slightly when she requested it, but she put it so reasonably that he just couldn't refuse. After all, she argued politely, a man of his noble and godly stature should be seen to be kind and considerate to his staff. It was an act of charity, she pointed out and he had to agree. The cook, Polly, and general maid, Kitty, were delighted.

Meanwhile in Peterborough town, life continued as normal. Whilst Rachel had been ill there had been much public consternation at the amount of gambling among the French prisoners of war at Norman Cross camp. They gambled so much that they literally lost the clothes off their backs, for their soldiers' uniforms had to be used to pay off their debts. The French authorities complained that the English were making their captives go naked, but that was far from the truth. So it was that the prisoners were now clothed in a brightly coloured prison uniform – a yellow suit and jacket, red waistcoat and grey cap. All in all, they looked more like canary birds than soldiers. When she went past the prison market whilst out buying supplies for the house, Rachel could hardly fail to notice them. In the sunshine the colours were quite dazzling.

A few weeks later however it seemed that they'd all disappeared for some reason. Kitty told them all the local gossip in the kitchen one evening, as they finally got the chance to relax, having cleared up the dinner things:

'Seems there's a terrible epidemic up at the camp. Typhus, so they say. Anyway, those Frenchies are dying in their thousands they reckon, and the council here told 'em they'd better keep

42

away from the town. We don't want it round 'ere.'

They certainly didn't. Typhus was a killer and no mistake. Whole populations were regularly devastated by it. Headache, stomach pain, fever – it was not to be wished on anyone, even if they were the enemy.

'Serves 'em right,' said Polly, who was sat in a worn-out easy chair by the fire. 'They shouldn't even be here, if you ask me. Do you know they've been gambling and fighting? The whole area's gone downhill since they been here.'

Rachel couldn't quite agree though she kept her views to herself. To her way of thinking Peterborough hadn't exactly been a haven of respectability before the soldiers arrived, so it didn't make much difference really. In fact, she thought, the town had improved somewhat recently.

In the early days of her new housekeeping job Rachel did find one thing which made life difficult – she wasn't able to read or write. She could understand figures, add up and check bills but words were a mystery to her. She was privately worried what might happen when it came to reading letters from tradesmen or the like. Rachel hid it well but there was a fear growing inside her like a canker that one day she might not be able to cope.

A couple of months after she started a crisis arose which proved Rachel's fears to be justified. Mrs Green came to Rachel asking her to arrange a dinner party for some friends of hers. She handed Rachel a piece of paper with all the details on it.

'Please sort this out for me; I'm sure you will manage as well as you usually do.' said her mistress and drifted off upstairs again, like a whisp of air.

Rachel retreated to the safety of her housekeeper's den before anyone could notice her tears. If her employers found out that she couldn't read, she knew she'd be dismissed. Furthermore, if the other staff knew, she'd be a laughing stock. Their respect for her would vanish like sunshine on a rainy day. Rachel peered at the paper trying to make sense of the unknown symbols. It might as well have been Egyptian hieroglyphics for all she knew. It meant nothing to her. Panic seized her and she couldn't think what to do. Her own family were no more literate than herself, none of them having had the opportunity of schooling. Then suddenly it came to her.

Rose Briggs, she thought. Maybe she could help me. I know she can read and write.

That afternoon Rachel made an excuse to go out, and secretly visited her friend. Going back to her old place of work was strange, but everyone was glad to see her and welcomed her warmly. To her surprise, Betty even made her a cup of tea. Emily had blossomed into a confident kitchen maid and together with Rachel's replacement, Lizzie, they made a good team. Rose was busy at first but made time as soon as she could for her friend.

'Come into my room,' she said leading the way. 'I hope all is well? You look distressed. What's wrong?'

Rachel poured out her troubles, grateful yet again for a friendly ear. Rose was only too happy to read the document to Rachel, but they decided then and there, between them, that Rachel would have to learn the basics of reading. Mrs Briggs promised to help.

'It looks really difficult,' said Rachel doubtfully.

'All you need is a few useful words,' Rose replied. 'If you can recognise those then you can guess the rest. I'll teach you.'

So, a series of furtive lessons began, once a week for a few weeks. Rachel practised and learnt fast, words for food, words for cleaning, words for work. What's more she felt happier and more confident because of it. She certainly couldn't read fluently but she could get by, and it got easier as time went on. As for writing she tried hard but holding the quill was difficult for her. Her fingers were still scarred and painful at times from the lasting effects of her illness. The ink went everywhere and just seemed to come out in large blots. The blank sky of the paper developed dark clouds which meant nothing. Well, you can't have everything, she thought and was satisfied.

Rachel settled into her new role happily now. She was popular with her staff who found her to be fair minded and reasonable. She expected a lot from them but gave her all in return. Her persona at work, like so many people, was confident and capable, completely unlike her own deeply insecure, introverted personality which was hidden from them all. Only a small handful of people really knew her, but maybe that's the same for everyone, she thought. Real knowledge of another's soul only happened with true love and she hadn't found that yet. Maybe she never would.

Chapter 5

1807

Charles Le Boucher sighed. He hated this time of day, for it was the time when he had to pack up his small market stall and return to the prison. He'd been there three years now, since being captured in 1804, and even though he had been given parole, he still hadn't got used to it. The clang of the prison gates behind him, each time he returned, made him feel desperate, like a caged wild animal.

What had he done to deserve it? he thought. Nothing, except do his duty for his country, and look where it had got him.

Across the way at the fruit and vegetable stall opposite, Charles saw a woman, obviously a housekeeper from her attire. She wore the usual grey striped silk dress and had a bunch of keys at her waist. Yet something about her caught his eye, though he couldn't say why.

Hearing a slight noise behind her, Rachel (for it was she) turned and for a brief moment their eyes met, then she turned back to the trader to finish negotiating her purchases.

Rachel had been working for Reverend Tutte for 6 years now, and once again, she was beginning to wonder where her life was going. The promised transformation hadn't quite materialised, though there had been certain improvements. She could read to a certain extent; she was capable and confident in her job and popular with her work colleagues. She kept in close contact with her family, in particular her niece Sarah, who was now married with two young children. Her nephew Edward had joined the militia, along with his older brother James, and Rachel worried about them both frequently. They were both abroad at present trying to defeat Napoleon's army. Rachel's sister Elizabeth was feeling her age now, as she was somewhat older, but on the whole she kept well.

Sadly, their mother had finally passed away a couple of years ago. Rachel still felt so guilty because she hadn't been able to be there at the time. She had known her mother was ill but hadn't realised it was as critical as it was. On the day it happened she had been out and about in town, running errands and settling bills for her master, not knowing that she would never speak to her mother again.

'Don't blame yourself,' Elizabeth had said. 'You didn't know. You were working. What else could you have done?'

Still the feelings of regret haunted her, and it took many months before she could put them aside.

Brothers Henry and William Alderman were both doing fairly well in business, but she saw little of them or their families. Their mother's funeral had been the last time all the family had been together. Now that their parents had both passed on, there was nothing to connect them all anymore.

Rachel's only real friend, Rose Briggs, had recently had to give up her housekeeper's post due to continuing ill health. Rachel visited her often, trying to ensure that her friend had everything she needed, but was concerned that she was going downhill. Now that she was no longer working Rose had had to move into a local alms house run by the town estates charity. It was small but well maintained and was better than the poorhouse, which was a large grey institution built of stone and as cold as the grave.

It was a week later when Charles saw Rachel again. It seemed she shopped there regularly. This time she looked over at his stall as she arrived, and he tipped his cap to her respectfully. She nodded in acknowledgement and then returned to her task. Nothing was said but human contact had been made. Rachel noticed a large well-built man, not handsome by any means, but striking in a way. His face showed strength of character in every line. Sad to see him in such ridiculously bright clothes, she thought, then forgot all about him.

Peterborough market was a colourful place, a melting pot of various cultures and backgrounds. Aside from the prisoners of war, there were British soldiers in uniform, local traders, tinkers, farmers, gypsies and even people with darker skins who Rachel initially stared at in wonder. She'd heard about natives from other lands being traded like commodities by the British government but had never come across them until recently. They scared her at first but then she began to feel sorry for them. After all they were just people like herself, being used and (often) abused to suit their masters' needs. When the slave trade was abolished in March that year Rachel could only think it a good thing.

This time the marketplace was very busy. People were jostling to get to the stall, and she had to queue up. As she neared the front, she suddenly became acutely aware of someone close by her. She could hear their breathing and feel their body heat next to her. It was then that Rachel heard the stallholder saying in a gruff voice:

'What do you want? You better have some money on you.'

For a moment Rachel thought he was talking to her, but then

she realised that it was directed at the person next to her. She risked a furtive glance in their direction and saw the man from the stall opposite. Clad all in yellow and red, the man stood out in the crowd, his long dark hair tied back loosely in a ponytail, his figure tall and strong.

'Pardon, Monsieur,' he replied in a French accent, 'but this lady was here before me. Please.'

He indicated Rachel. She blushed.

'Have you got any money on you?' the stallholder growled at him again. 'If not, clear off and stop wasting my time!'

'Certainly, I have the money,' he said in broken English. 'See,' and Rachel heard the clink of coins. 'But please to serve the lovely lady first.'

'Humph!' the stallholder grunted. 'Well Madam, how can I help you?'

By now Rachel had lost all her customary composure, and her normal calm façade had shattered into pieces, like china falling on a stone floor. She stammered and struggled her way through her purchase, quite unlike her usual self. By the end of it she was flushed, perspiring and glad to escape. Throughout the encounter however, she was deeply conscious of the stranger next to her and all she could think of was that he had called her 'lovely'. No-one had ever said that about her before.

That night in bed it haunted her dreams – lovely, lovely, lovely – it echoed in her head over and over, and when she rose in the early hours there was a glow on her face that hadn't been there before.

Meanwhile Charles, blithely unaware of the effect he had had on her, returned sadly to the prison to ponder his lot. The few apples he had been able to purchase were sour and hard and had done little to assuage his longings. They were adequately fed in the prison camp, of course, but it was basic, plain fare, consisting mainly of beef, bread, potatoes and the dreaded cabbage. It was plentiful, but nothing like they were used to at home. Looking at the grey faces of his compatriots, Charles knew they needed more. His memories of French home cooking were distant now, but still at times he fancied he could smell garlic and olives, and his taste buds quivered at the thought of them.

Clambering into his hammock that night Charles thought of the unknown woman he had seen in the town. He'd been watching her from his stall, in spite of the fact that she was no great beauty. Something about her had struck him – an inner light, a depth of feeling rarely seen. He longed to find out more but doubted whether he would get the chance.

A week later it was Rachel's monthly day off and she had arranged to go shopping with her niece Sarah. There was a forthcoming birthday for Sarah's 4-year-old son, Jimmy, and Rachel wanted to get him a present. For some reason that day she dressed with special care, wearing her best day dress, lace shawl and a new lace cap. Sarah was very impressed when they met up and commented on it.

'You're looking very nice today, Aunty,' she said, then teased gently: 'Is there love in the air or something?'

'Don't be silly!' replied Rachel but she blushed anyway.

It was a beautiful summer day, bright but fresh with blue sky and birds singing. It almost seemed as if it were newly laundered. They walked around the shops in the town but after some time of finding nothing suitable, Rachel suggested they try the market.

'There are lots of different traders there. We may find something unusual for him.'

There were certainly many stalls there, but they headed slowly, inexorably towards the place where Rachel knew she would find the Frenchman. It was like a magnet drawing her in. Sarah, of course, was oblivious to her aunt's impulses and gaily went along with it all. She was surprised, however, that Rachel had found nothing she liked so far.

They turned the corner and there he was. Charles was sat on an old wooden crate, his wares spread out on the ground. These were delicately carved toys and ornaments, made from animal bones which he had managed to obtain from the kitchens at the camp. He looked up as they approached and raised his cap politely. For a moment he didn't recognise Rachel in different clothes, but then he realised and smiled broadly.

'May I help you, Mam`selles?' he asked.

Rachel gazed at him, never having seen a man who stirred her feelings so strangely before. She suddenly felt very shy and for a moment could hardly talk. Her face flushed crimson and her hands were trembling. What a fool she must look! Sarah came to her rescue, unknowingly however, by starting to pick up and look at the objects for sale.

'Rachel,' she declared. 'These are lovely. Do look!'

Rachel turned her attention to them and had to add her admiration. They were fine and beautiful, and her attention was captured. In particular she was taken by a toy ship, which she thought would be just right for young Jimmy. This distraction relieved her shyness and helped her regain her composure. Feeling brave enough to speak, she asked:

'How much is this, please? It's a lovely piece of work.'

'Why merci, Mam'selle, thank you, I mean,' replied Charles and he named a very reasonable price.

'That seems very cheap,' Rachel said.

'A special deal for you,' he replied smiling at her. 'We have already met, yes?'

'Well, yes, I suppose we have,' she admitted, smiling back, in spite of herself.

'Have you?' asked Sarah, surprised.

'Just in passing,' said Rachel, blushing again. 'I usually get the vegetables for the house at the stall over the way.' She paused. 'But we haven't been introduced,' she added.

'Charles Le Boucher, at your service, Mam'selle,' he said and raised his hat again.

'Rachel Alderman,' she said, 'and this is my niece, Sarah.'

She gave him her hand to shake but he raised it to his lips to kiss it before she could pull it away.

'Sir!' she exclaimed. 'Really!'

'My apologies, Mam'selle. It is how we do things in France. I have forgot myself.'

'Come on Rachel,' said Sarah. 'It's not proper to stay here talking to these French prisoners. Let's just buy this and go.' She turned away and walked off to the next stall.

Rachel paid Charles, embarrassed, and he packed up the toy in silence. As he passed over the package, however, their hands briefly touched, and Rachel felt a tingle go up her spine. She looked into his eyes and smiled.

'I am so sorry,' Charles insisted again. 'Please forgive me.'

'It's alright,' she replied. 'I understand. There's no harm done. Please take no notice of my niece. Her brothers are at the war, and she is very worried about them.'

'Quel dommage. What a pity.' Charles said.

'Yes,' said Rachel. 'It's a hard time for everyone.'

They parted cordially and she moved away to join Sarah.

'I can't think why you are talking to that man!' her niece said, crossly. 'He's one of the enemy, you know!'

'Yes, I know, but he can't help it. Anyway, we've got a lovely present for Jimmy.' Then she changed the subject: 'I'm thirsty. Let's go and take some tea.'

Sarah was pacified, the sun shone, and the day became calm again. Nevertheless, Rachel couldn't stop thinking about the meeting. She still felt the touch of the stranger's lips on her hand, and in her mind, she could see his smile. What had happened to her? She had never felt so alive.

Chapter 6

Over the next few days Rachel's initial feelings of elation gave way to more sombre emotions of self-doubt, paranoia and even fear. She questioned things in her mind, endlessly, keeping her awake at night.

Why should he look at her? she asked herself. Anyway, nothing could come of it. He was just teasing her, just like Tommy. No-one wanted her. Why would they? She was so plain, even ugly, she thought. Perhaps it was all a game, maybe he was a rogue out to trap her. Then again, maybe she'd misread the whole situation – she had no experience of men. He was probably just being polite, that's all it was.

By the time Rachel next visited the market she had convinced herself that it would do no good to pursue the friendship and that she should just ignore him completely. She steeled herself as she approached and tried hard not to look in the direction of the Frenchman's humble stall. Nevertheless, their eyes met briefly as she came down the path. Charles raised his hat to her, smiling, but she deliberately turned away and got on with her business, aware all the time of his presence just the other side of the aisle. Hardening her heart, Rachel collected her purchases and left quickly, but even so she couldn't fail to notice the look of disappointment on Charles' face as she swept by.

When she was alone in bed that night her tears fell, and she realised that she had been rude and unpleasant. No-one would forgive a snub like that. The friendship was finished before it had even begun. And with that thought she cried even more. What harm would it have done to be friends with him? It was innocent enough after all and not likely to lead to anything else.

On her half day off Rachel visited Rose again, finding her worryingly weak and frail this time. After fixing her some soup and making up the fire afresh they sat and talked. To her surprise, Rachel found herself telling her friend about the meeting. Rose listened quietly, making no judgement until Rachel finally asked for her opinion.

'What do you think? Should I speak to him? As Sarah said, he is the enemy, but somehow, I can't quite see it that way.'

Rose smiled gently.

'Rachel, my dear, I think you have made your own decision. In your heart, I can tell that you want to get to know him. Besides, what harm can it do? It's always better to make friends if you have the chance. Ask yourself which feels right for you – to despise him, or to like him? Trust your instincts.'

'He seems nice,' said Rachel thoughtfully, 'and I want to be friends with him, but I'm not good with people, as you know.'

'It can't hurt to pass the time of day,' Rose said. 'Just a smile or a 'hello' – it's not asking a lot. Why not try it?'

So, the next time Rachel visited the market she was eager to make amends for her former rudeness. Imagine her disappointment, therefore, when she found merely an empty space where Charles' stall had been. Distracted by her feelings she ended up buying far too many potatoes for the house, and no carrots (which made life difficult the following week). Wandering the various aisles of the marketplace, she searched to see if he had moved somewhere else, but there was no sign of him. It was then that she realised that there was an absence of all the usual, brightly clad Frenchmen from the scene. She wondered what had happened. Maybe they were all being sent home?

Eventually on a pretext of wanting to buy something, Rachel asked one of the market stewards if they knew anything.

'Oh yes, lady. They've all been kept back at the camp. Didn't you hear? There was a mass break out a couple of days ago. They caught 'em all, mind. Found 700 weapons, so it's said! You can bet they'll be punished good and proper. Serves 'em right, French bastards! They should hang the lot of them!'

Rachel shuddered at the thought but thanked the man and turned away. She'd rarely been past the prison depot, (it was just outside the town), but now it seemed to draw her there and she found a detour which took her that way. Gazing up at the formidable metal gates, she wondered what life was like in there. It was a huge site, heavily fenced and ringed with guards. One of them approached her as she stood there deep in thought.

'Can I help you, Miss?'

'What's happened to all the soldiers?' she asked. 'I hear they tried to escape.'

'Getting what they deserve, I'm pleased to say. Floggings, half rations and the like. Just let 'em see how they like the black hole!'

'The black hole – what's that?' she asked, horrified.

'Our punishment block, Miss. No windows, all dark and silent-sends 'em half mad, it does!'

He laughed, but there was no humour, only a cruel pleasure in other people's misfortunes.

'They'll all suffer for this outrage. There'll be no more outings to the town for a while, that's for sure! That'll teach 'em.'

Sadly, Rachel headed home. So that was that, then, she thought.

Meanwhile within one of the many blockhouses, each built to house 500 men, Charles continued peeling enormous heaps of potatoes, wishing he was outside in the town as usual. All parole had been cancelled for the time being. His thoughts wandered briefly to Rachel, but he tried to dismiss them. After all, hadn't she ignored him last time he saw her?

Rumours that the outer wooden stockade was to be replaced with a sturdy wall had sparked the flames of the huge escape attempt the previous week. The inmates knew that they'd never be able to get past a wall, so some felt it was their last chance. They'd rushed at it, en masse, knocking down a whole section in their enthusiasm, only to be confronted by yet another fence and a ditch.

Stupid, thought Charles to himself. It was obvious it was never going to work. What were they thinking? They'd all been rounded up before they got more than a dozen yards. Now the ring leaders were languishing in the dreaded 'black hole' and the rest of them were being made to suffer in various ways.

Charles could stand the short rations, the beatings and the hard physical labour, but not being allowed to make their usual crafts frustrated him. He had never felt creative until he came here but being locked in had provided him with time on his hands and a need to do something useful. A ready supply of cattle bone from their daily diet had enabled the men to experiment, and to his surprise Charles had found a skill and a pleasure he had never guessed at. Model ships were his favourite thing to make, each one lovingly carved and all slightly different. The markings of the bone made every item delightfully unique. Of course, the extra money from the sales helped, but he took most satisfaction in talking to the customers and seeing the admiration on their faces as they handled the goods.

Besides the blockhouses, there were of course the necessary ablutions, and a large guard house at the centre, well manned and exceedingly well armed. (Charles had heard there were cannons). There was also a hospital, a barracks and of course, an exercise yard, where they performed routinely boring and meaningless activities designed to keep them fit. On the plus side, prisoners were offered the chance to learn to read and write, and even fencing and dancing were available at times. Many of the inmates spent their hours less constructively, however, in gambling. Charles had been known to indulge in this occasionally, but seeing how much money others lost, he was wary and strict with himself. While it could be a thrill, it was also hopelessly addictive, and he decided he didn't need that kind of excitement. Maybe when he was young and foolish, he would have been more easily swayed, but he was over 40 now and mature enough to resist.

Usually, the prison population was around the 3000 mark but it fluctuated as prisoners came and went. There were many different nationalities, and even some women and children amongst them, as well as a few unfortunate civilians, who were just in the wrong place at the wrong time! Sometimes inmates were exchanged for British prisoners and went home, though these were usually the Dutch or Spanish soldiers, not the French, who the authorities still considered very dangerous. Some died (mostly from disease) and some (occasionally) escaped. New captives appeared all the time, marching in, as Charles himself had done, from places as far away as Portsmouth. He remembered the dreary trudge which went on for days, along rough cart tracks, pitted with holes and caked with mud, followed by a cramped ride on a barge from Kings Lynn. Charles' knowledge of the geography of England was limited but he knew they must now be many miles away from the sea. At home he had lived on a farm near the coast of France, (Brittany to be exact), and had often smelt the salt in the air from the nearby ocean. Then he had been conscripted into the French navy and had experienced the smell of the wild sea first hand. There was no such tang in the air here and he wondered where they were. He knew the nearest town was called Peterborough but where that was in relation to London, let alone France, he had no idea. He felt stranded, cast off, adrift in a strange country where he was regarded only as 'the enemy.'

It wouldn't have been so bad, but besides the many disciplined and highly trained military troops guarding them, there were local civilian staff. They were mostly employed as 'turn keys' (prison warders), keeping the doors locked and secure, and maintaining the daily routine. Some of them were brutal thugs who took every delight in tormenting the prisoners. Beatings and abuse were common, though officially frowned upon, and it was hard to get along with these men. One in particular, Alexander Halliday, seemed to have a mission in life to make the prisoners' time there as miserable as possible. He was a mean looking, shrivelled up man, with thin grey hair and a bony face, like a skeleton. His body seemed to be permanently clenched in some kind of inner anger, which he was resolved to take out on everyone he encountered. Maybe he had suffered his own misfortunes in life which had made him the way he was, but even so there was no excuse for his incessant, mocking cruelty.

Unfortunately, Charles had soon felt his wrath. One day, not long after he had arrived, he had refused a piece of bread because it was stale and smelt musty. Halliday had pounced on him with glee:

'Oh, high and mighty, are we? Not good enough for you, is it? I suppose you're going to go and tell your wonderful committee, are you? Well, see what it's like to go without, then, Frenchie!'

Consequently, Charles received only half rations for the next few days, until he was so hungry that he was desperate and forced to beg. He pleaded with his captor for a morsel of something – anything!

Halliday laughed at him.

'Not so proud now, are we? Here take this!'

He flung him the hardest, driest piece of bread that he could find, and made Charles eat it, even though it nearly choked him. Briefly, Charles considered going to the prison committee and telling them. They kept a watch on the quality of the food and reported back to the agent if anything was inadequate, but he knew that this would mean even more abuse from his tormenter. So instead, Charles did his best to avoid the man, but Halliday appeared to search him out on every opportunity, just to bully him. Silently Charles swore to himself that if he ever got the chance, he would teach him a lesson he would never forget.

Two weeks went by since the escape attempt and luckily the guards soon got tired of looking after the entire prison population all the time. They quickly took to grumbling about the extra hours for no extra pay, so in the end those in charge decided something had to be done. A limited return to outside visits was to be allowed for those of good conduct and who had not been involved in any escape attempt so far. In both these instances Charles was fully qualified, and so the following Monday he was back in the marketplace once more.

Rachel's spirits leapt when she saw him, and she rushed over to his stall impulsively. Suddenly she realised that she had no idea what to say to him. Should she apologise for her rudeness? Should she pretend it had never happened? What if he turned her away?

In the end her words all came out in a rush.

'You're back! I'm glad. Are you well?'

Charles smiled. He was pleased to see her and bore no ill will.

'Mam'selle Alderman, I am well, merci. It is good to be back here again in the, how do you say it? Open air?'

'Fresh air,' she replied, smiling back. Then she blushed, remembering her former behaviour.

'Last time I saw you,' she said awkwardly, 'I, well, I mean, I didn't mean to, well you know-'

Charles took her hand gently and raised it to his lips but did not kiss it.

'It is all forgot, Mam'selle. It is of no matter.'

'I'm sorry!' she blurted out. 'Really.'

'It is of no matter, Mam'selle,' he repeated. 'Please to forget it.'

They talked a little and Rachel admired the objects on his stall, including some strange rectangular objects with coloured dots on them. She wondered what they were, and Charles explained.

'We call them dominoes, Mam'selle. Do you not have them here in your country? They are for the playing of a game. It is popular in France.'

'I have never heard of it before,' she said. 'These things are all so beautiful. You are very talented. Where did you learn to make them?'

'Only here, Mam'selle, in prison.'

For a moment Charles lost his usual composure.

'Before this, all I did was farming. I had no time for such things.'

'Were you long in the army?' Rachel asked. 'Before you were captured, I mean.'

Then she became embarrassed at herself for asking such personal questions.

'Sorry, you don't have to tell me.'

'But I am most happy to, Mam'selle. We are friends, no? Friends should talk, should they not?'

'Well, yes, I think so,' she stammered.

'Actually, I was in the navy, which I was forced to join in 1803,' he told her. 'But very soon my ship was hit by cannons and damaged beyond repair. Those of us who survived were captured and sent here. I am just lucky because I was a second officer (sadly, the man before me drowned) and that means I get some parole.'

Charles had always felt bad about this. A violent squall had sent their flimsy ship pitching and tossing, flinging three men to the hungry waves, never to be seen again. His promotion (such as it was) had made him feel guilty and unclean, as if he had had a hand in the unfortunate officer's demise. The only good that had come out of it was this partial freedom, for which he was thankful.

He sighed, remembering.

'I still have to reside at the depot. I can only leave during certain hours of the daytime.'

'So, you've been here a long time then?' she asked, surprised.

'Yes, four years in prison,' he agreed. 'It is long, yes, but time outside helps. That is why the last three weeks were so difficult.'

They chatted a bit more, then Rachel remembered that she needed to get back to her duties. Taking her leave of him, she promised to visit him again. She couldn't really say why, but it was good to have a new friend. That was all it could ever be, of course, but what was wrong with that?

Chapter 7

Summer slowly turned into early autumn, and with the changing of the seasons so their friendship grew. Each time Rachel visited the market she found time to chat with Charles. It was only polite conversation to start with, about the weather and the like, but soon it moved to more personal subjects such as family. It was only a few weeks since Charles had reappeared from the prison lockdown when Rachel found out, with a shock, that he was married.

The conversation started pleasantly enough.

'How are you today, Mam`selle Rachel?' Charles enquired smiling.

'Very well, thank you,' she replied. 'Yesterday I went to see my sister Elizabeth White, who I haven't seen for a while. We had a lovely day, catching up on everything.'

'Tell me about her,' he said. 'Is she like you?'

'Oh no, she's married with a family – something I have never managed to do,' she added, with regret. 'But Elizabeth has always been most pleasing to the eye and very sociable, so it's not surprising. No, she's not like me at all.'

'What do you mean?'

'I'm not good with people.' Rachel blushed, just thinking about it. 'And then, well, she is quite beautiful - which I'll never be.'

'Mam`selle!' Charles exclaimed, 'do not be so hard on yourself. If you do not mind me saying, excuse my impertinence, but you seem a very fine lady to me.'

Rachel glowed both with pleasure and embarrassment.

'You are too kind, Sir,' she murmured.

To change the subject away from herself, she asked:

'And what family do you have? Any brothers or sisters?'

'Why yes, a brother, also in the navy, two sisters, and of course my wife's family.'

Wife? Rachel stared at him. It had never occurred to her that he could be married. An overwhelming feeling of disappointment choked her, and she struggled not to show it. Her stammer suddenly returned, as it usually did when her confidence was dented.

'Your w..w..wife,' she swallowed hard. 'What is she like? She must miss you.'

Charles laughed; a hard, bitter laugh.

'I doubt it! I think she will be glad to be rid of me.'

'Surely not!' exclaimed Rachel, then losing her composure again she stammered: 'Is that the time? I must be getting back. Please excuse me.'

'Of course, Mam`selle. Until next time we meet, may good fortune attend you.'

He bowed slightly. Rachel did her best to respond politely and then sped off, before she could let herself down by bursting into tears.

Somehow, she held herself together until later. The other staff found her quiet and tense that afternoon, but they never said anything. Polly did remark to Kitty, privately, that she thought there was something wrong, but as Kitty said:

'I guess it ain't our business. She `as these moods sometimes.'

'Well, she's a good `un anyway, so what do it matter to us?' Polly replied, 'but still I don't like to see `er so down in the dumps.'

Unaware of their conversation, Rachel was pleased to think that she had hidden her distress from them. After all she had her position to think of. Finally, alone at the end of the day, she gave way to her feelings.

Married? Of course, he was. Why hadn't she thought of that? A man of his age and character – why wouldn't he be? Had she really thought that they had any chance of a relationship anyway? He was a foreign prisoner of war, and she was a lonely spinster. She had told herself, often enough, that they could only ever be friends, but in her heart, she had hoped for more. How stupid she was. What a fool!

Meanwhile, Charles dealt with the painful memories that the mention of his wife had brought to the surface again. He kept trying to put it all behind him, but it kept returning to haunt him. What could he do?

Over the next few days Rachel fought to get her feelings under control. She would conquer this, she told herself firmly. She would still be friends with Charles. There was no harm in it. On the next occasion she saw him she kept the talk light and friendly, asking him how he was being treated and if he was well. Charles told her stories about the prison and his fellow inmates, making her laugh with his anecdotes. A shadow passed over his face when talking about the warders, but Rachel didn't notice. When they parted, she privately congratulated herself for keeping her composure, and she resolved to continue with this in the future.

One breezy day in September, Rachel found to her discomfort, that Charles was not, as was usual, alone on his humble stall. He was surrounded by several other prisoners (evident from their colourful uniforms) all of whom were talking loudly in French. Rachel approached warily, aware that some of the men were looking at her. Charles said something to one of them in his own language and they all guffawed raucously. Rachel's immediate thought was that they were all laughing at her. She couldn't say why, but it had always been the same; each time people were making merry near her, she felt it was at her expense. Charles gestured towards her and two of the men turned to look in her direction. One of them nudged him in a knowing way and there was more laughter.

Rachel flushed and hurried away, unaware that Charles was looking annoyed. She thought she heard him call after her, but she did not stop to find out.

How could he? Obviously, she was just a figure of fun to him – a sad English spinster, an old maid, desperate for a friend.

Tormented by thoughts of this Rachel was in no mood to sort out her staff's problems when she returned to the vicarage, but there she found Kitty in tears and Polly stomping around in a huff.

'That stupid girl's gone and broken the Missus's favourite vase!' Polly declared to Rachel, pointing at a distraught Kitty.

'Well, what of it?' questioned Rachel. 'Surely it's not the end of the world?'

The cook continued.

'The Missus saw and threw a right fit, then she comes down 'ere and tells us we're both (both, mind!) to go without pay until it's replaced. Ain't my fault, so I don't see that's fair. I told her so 'n all but she told me if I didn't like it, I could clear off! As for 'er, (she gestured at the maid) she just cries and cries, can't get no sense out of 'er.'

Shifting into 'work' mode, Rachel soothed and calmed the two servants, making tea and promising to speak to the Mistress about it. At least they were all on speaking terms again and Kitty had just about ceased her tears by the time Rachel went upstairs. Luckily, she found the Mistress with the Reverend in the drawing room and knew that this meant that the encounter was likely to be an easier affair than it would otherwise have been. Reverend Tutte was a kind and understanding gentleman, even if his sister was somewhat given to hysterics.

'Mistress Green,' she began, 'I'm terribly sorry to hear of the misfortune with the vase.'

'Misfortune!' the fine lady exclaimed. 'It was a most monstrous deed!'

'Yes, of course,' agreed Rachel in her most pacifying voice, 'but accidents do happen unfortunately.'

'It was sheer carelessness!' the widow declared. 'She should have been looking where she was going.'

'Perhaps you could tell me exactly what happened,' said Rachel, 'then I could talk to her about it.'

It turned out that Kitty had been dusting but had unfortunately tripped over the edge of the carpet, which was badly frayed just there. Rachel had previously informed her mistress that this needed renewal, but money was tight, and it hadn't been done. As Mrs Green talked it through, she began to realise that Kitty hadn't been entirely to blame. She faltered and hesitated.

'Well, perhaps I have been a bit hasty. I was just so upset. My late husband bought me that vase.'

'I'm so sorry,' Rachel murmured sympathetically. 'Is there no way it can be fixed?'

The Reverend cut in at this point, enthusiastically.

'Well, I think maybe it could. Perhaps, Mrs Alderman, you could sort this out?'

He brought out the pieces and she examined them.

'Yes, I think so,' she agreed.

Mrs Green had regained her composure.

'Oh, I'd be so grateful,' she said. 'Can you arrange it?'

'Of course, there's only one thing, Ma'am, and that's the staff. The cook is truly upset by having her wages cut, and I doubt whether she will be able to manage without pay. She has an aged mother to look after, and Kitty can be a foolish girl, I know, but she's a good worker and I wouldn't want to lose either of them.'

'Lose them!' exclaimed the Reverend. 'Certainly not! Letitia, dear, I think we must be more lenient.'

Mrs Green agreed that her original decision was somewhat in error and dropped the idea. It was decided that Kitty alone would make a small contribution towards the cost of repair, and Rachel was satisfied. The other staff were impressed by the results of her intervention and ended the day happily.

Alone in her housekeepers room however Rachel finally had time to think over the incident at the market. If only she could deal with outside people in the same calm, efficient manner as she did at work, but it was no good. She was a prisoner of her own fears and insecurities. Why should it matter? she reasoned and tried to harden her heart against Charles. Nevertheless, she tossed and turned in her bed that night.

For the next couple of visits to the market Rachel studiously avoided any eye contact with the Frenchman on his stall. On the second occasion, however she heard him call out to her:

'Mam'selle, please! Are you alright?'

Her heart told her to turn and reply but she ignored it and hurried off. Meanwhile Charles was confused and hurt. What had happened to their friendship? He suddenly realised that he valued it more than he had thought. There were friends at the prison, of course, but no-one like her. The image of her haunted him in his dreams at night. He looked forward to their encounters and now something was clearly wrong. He knew he had to make it right and vowed that next time he saw her he wouldn't let her escape until she gave him an explanation.

Unfortunately, his main tormenter, Halliday, used his thoughtfulness the following day to bully and chastise him. When Charles missed some of the floor he was supposed to be mopping, the vindictive 'turn-key' made him do it over and over again. On the fourth time Charles' patience finally snapped and he turned on the man, shouting at him, refusing to do any more. Halliday responded harshly, shoving Charles roughly against the wall and adding in some brutal whacks with his stick for good measure. In pain, but not cowed, Charles retreated to the block house, only to be dragged out again and put in the 'black hole' overnight. The solitude and the lonely darkness only served to increase Charles' personal misery. In there, everything seemed so suffocatingly close and intense that there was no escape from it.

Thankfully by the following week Charles was out and back on his stall again as Rachel came into sight. This time he was not to be put off, and he instantly got up, took her by the arm and led her off to one side.

'Sir!' she exclaimed. 'What are you doing? Leave me alone.'

Frightened that someone would hear her and call an officer, Charles pleaded.

Mam'selle,' he begged, 'please listen. I am forlorn. Why will you not speak to me now? At least I deserve the explaining.'

Rachel smiled, in spite of herself, at his awkward use of English.

'I think you mean 'explanation',' she said, 'well alright then.' She paused and blushed nervously. Then she blurted out: 'I don't like being laughed at.

'Laughed at?' Charles queried. 'What do you mean?'

Rachel felt herself growing angry as she remembered.

'Yes! I was just a figure of fun to you and your friends, wasn't I? I know I'm a lonely old maid, not much to look at and no use to anyone, but I will not be humiliated like that!'

'My friends?' said Charles, confused.

'Yes, a couple of weeks ago. You were all laughing at me, I know it.'

'Non, non! You are most wrong, Mam'selle. How can you think that I would do that? My friends were admiring you and teasing me. They said that you must be my woman, my mistress. I am sorry! I told them you are a decent respectable lady and they laughed at me, not you. They called me a fool for not making you mine. I must apologise for their low morals and poor conduct. Please forgive me.'

Rachel realised with embarrassment that her own paranoia had led her astray.

'Really?' she said. 'You mean it?'

'Naturellement,' Charles declared. 'No-one will ever treat you like that, with me around. I would not let them. You are a fine lady. We are still friends, no?'

'Yes, of course,' she replied smiling. 'I owe you an apology. The trouble is that I have had some bad times in the past and it has made it difficult for me to trust people.'

Charles released her arm gently.

'Why do we not go for a walk by the river?' he suggested. 'It is a pleasant afternoon, and we could sit down and talk.'

Rachel hesitated barely a moment before allowing herself to be led to a quiet seat by the Nene, where they talked as freely as the running water. For some reason she felt able to open up to him in a way she never had to anyone before.

Eventually Rachel suddenly remembered her duties.

'I must be getting back,' she said, 'but it has been so nice being here, talking to you. I've never really had many friends.'

'You will always have a friend in me, Mam'selle Rachel,' Charles replied, 'but to speak truly, I wish it could be more.'

The he kissed her hand gently and walked off back to his part of the marketplace, leaving her with her thoughts in a whirl.

More! No man had ever wanted more of her. How could it be? How could this be happening?

Rachel returned to the vicarage in a daze.

Chapter 8

As he returned to the prison, Charles silently cursed himself. What was he thinking? Surely now she would refuse to have anything more to do with him. And what about his wife? That was another thing altogether.

Meanwhile Rachel was virtually dancing on air. Her spirits were high, and dreams of love filled her head. At least, that was until she visited her niece Sarah on her monthly day off. They were very close; Rachel having been like a mother to Sarah and her siblings whilst they were growing up. Her brother-in-law John had been married to Ellen for many years now, but his grown-up children still looked to Rachel for guidance and affection. Today Sarah was worried and depressed. She'd had a letter from her youngest brother Edward over in the West Indies. He was busy fighting the French for possession of certain small Caribbean territories and his regiment were having a terrible time of it, many being killed every day. Rations were short and disease was rife. Edward's best friend Jonas had just died from one of the many unknown fevers that lurked there in wait for them. What's more, he had lost touch with their brother James who had been shipped out elsewhere: the rumour was that he was in Russia or maybe Spain – no-one seemed very clear about it.

'Oh, what can we do?' said Sarah, desperately wringing her hands. 'Aunty Rachel, it's so unfair. The French are an evil force. They have no honour – none! Torturers and murderers!

Barbarians – the lot of them!'

Rachel felt embarrassed and awkward. Perhaps Sarah was right about some of them, but she knew Charles was different. She felt it deep down in her soul.

'War brings out the worst in people,' she began. 'Maybe they are not all as bad.'

'How can you say that?' Sarah flared up angrily. 'Really Aunty, you don't understand anything!'

Rachel hated to argue with anyone, let alone her beloved niece, so she said meekly:

'No, no, perhaps not. My knowledge is very limited.'

'Well, there you are then!' Sarah declared. 'Now help me write a letter to poor dear Edward. He will be glad to hear our news.'

Rachel tried, but the only news she had, certainly couldn't be shared. Her spirits sank and by the time she left Sarah she was in despair. Rather than head straight back she resolved to go and visit her friend Rose Briggs. The dear old lady always had a way of helping her see things clearly.

Rachel had always visited Rose regularly and had noted the elderly woman's sad decline lately. On this occasion she was alarmed to find her lying in bed, her hair unkempt on the pillow and her face pale and drawn.

'Rose, dear. Let me help tidy you up. How are you?'

She bustled around, propping up the pillows, brushing Rose's hair and fixing her some broth, but Rose could only manage a few mouthfuls.

'I'm fine,' said Rose, but her voice was croaky. 'Dear Rachel, you are very good to me. Sit down and then we can talk, it will do me more good than anything.'

'I don't want to tire you,' said Rachel, sitting on the edge of the bed. She could see that her friend was wasting away.

Rose patted her hand.

'You have a cloud over you, my dear. Tell me about it. A problem shared; you know.'

Rachel smiled. Dear old Rose, always thinking of others. If only there were more people like that.

'The thing is, well it's strange, difficult, but I think I'm in love!'

Rose gazed at her. 'With the French soldier you talked about before?' she asked.

'What?' gasped Rachel. 'But how? How did you know?'

'It's easy to see,' said Rose. 'I think it's been there all along.'

'But I know it's wrong,' continued Rachel. 'He's a prisoner, and then again, it's worse, I found out that he's married! Oh, what a mess!' A tear trickled down her face. 'And yet, and yet he says he likes me and wants to be more than just a friend. What should I do? Oh Rose! He's the enemy, it's all wrong. There's no future for us anyway.'

After this confused outpouring of emotion Rachel felt drained. It was all useless.

Rose was quiet for a few moments.

'Love is never wrong,' she said finally. 'It may be in the wrong place or the wrong time, but it is not wrong to love someone, believe me.' Her face looked sad. 'I loved a man once who went off overseas, but I was adamant I would not give myself to him, because I wanted to wait for us to be wed when he returned. But he never did. He was lost at sea. Now I wish I hadn't been so stubborn. Live for today, my dear. Take your chances as they happen and do not worry about the future. It may never come.'

'So, you think I should pursue this?' Rachel asked.

'Do what your heart tells you to do, my dear. People may tell you it's wrong; society may tell you it's wrong; but it's your life, your feelings. We only get one life, as far as we know. Make the most of it.'

'My family would be horrified,' replied Rachel. 'Sarah is so worried about Edward and James, out fighting in the war. I don't want to upset anyone. And my sister Elizabeth thinks the French are all dirty thieves and rogues as well. She's always complaining about them. Only the other day she found one of them of going through her rubbish and she reported him to one of the guards. I said that maybe they were just hungry, but she didn't see it that way.'

'But as you've discovered, my dear, you cannot judge a person just by their race. You must take them as you find them.'

'You're so right,' agreed Rachel, 'but you're the only one who will understand this. What should I do?'

'You must ask yourself some questions and answer them honestly. Do you want to keep seeing him? Do you want to know him better? Could you bear never to see him again?'

Rachel knew the answers to these instantly in her heart and decided that from then on, she would live for the moment, whatever that would bring.

She left Rose's humble alms house later than usual that day. The daylight was fast slipping away, and Rachel hurried along. Though the city was safer and cleaner than it used to be, thanks to the 'Improvement Programme', the streets of Peterborough were still no place for a lone woman in the evening (unless they were of a certain sort of course!). Absentmindedly giving a few coins to the usual street urchins, Rachel made every effort to avoid the regiment of rogues and ruffians who were assembling for their night-time duties. A large blousy looking woman jeered at her from an open doorway and a drunken British soldier shouted some obscenities in her direction. She was relieved therefore when she entered the quieter area around the Minster, where the vicarage was located. Shutting the servants' door safely behind her, she realised that she was one of the lucky ones. She had a decent job and a roof over her head, with reasonable employers, pleasant colleagues and a degree of respectability. Did she dare risk all that for a romantic liaison that could never have a future? To her amazement, she knew that the answer was yes.

A couple of days later Charles was surprised to see Rachel approaching his stall in the marketplace. Surprised because it wasn't her normal day or time to visit, and also because she was dressed in non-working clothes. He felt embarrassed all of a sudden, remembering their last meeting, and he fumbled and faltered whilst serving a large proportioned, well to do lady who was buying a carved dolls house from him.

'Do you want to sell this or not?' she demanded, getting annoyed.

'Mais oui! Apologies Madame. Here it is. Forgive me.'

She paid and went off, albeit rather huffily. Rachel came closer, feeling suddenly shy. She'd had it all clear in her head before she left home, but now she was here it was different.

'Mam'selle Rachel,' said Charles, 'I did not expect to see you today. Are you well?'

'Yes, indeed,' replied Rachel nervously. She started to stammer.

'I came to see you. I, I wanted to talk to you about …..' her voice trailed off and she found she was sweating.

'Mam'selle Rachel, I must apologise for anything I may have said to offend you last time we met. I was too forward, I am thinking, and you are upset. Please ignore what I said, it was a mistake.'

'A mistake!' Rachel looked crestfallen. 'So, you did not mean it?'

Charles hesitated and could not look her in the eye. 'I cannot say that Mam'selle. It would be, how you say it, a lie.'

Rachel blushed deeply and tried to say the words that she had rehearsed so often.

'I, well, I, that is, if you won't think badly of me, I wish…..'

'You do not need to explain, Mam'selle. I understand and can only apologise.'

'No, no, that's not it! I wish the same - there, I said it! I know it's foolish, but I can't help it.'

'Do you mean it?' he asked, incredulous.

Rachel nodded, scarcely able to speak. Then she hung her head in shame.

'Oh, but your wife – I must not say these things. You belong to another. You are married.' She paused, anxious.

There was a shadow on Charles' face.

'You do not need to worry about her,' he said in a strange voice. His face was full of pain.

'Well, I know, but one day you will return to her.'

'I need to explain,' Charles said, 'my wife and I are not happy together. I was persuaded to marry her by my father to save our farm. My father is the town mayor, but we have no money. The bank was threatening to take away everything we had. Eloise, my wife, she comes from a wealthy family, but she did not want to marry me; she loved another man. Her family forced her, in order to get the 'honour' of being related to the town mayor!'

He laughed drily, then continued.

'I have tried to make her happy, but she hates me. She has become bitter and angry with a vicious temper. When I left to join the navy, she told me she hoped I would get killed so that she would never have to see me again. I dread going back to her. War has, at least, served to get me away.'

He paused, studying Rachel's face.

'But it is true that one day, if I am spared, I will have to go home. There is no future for us, Mam'selle Rachel, and so I cannot ask for anything from you.'

'You do not need to ask,' she said impulsively, and her eyes shone. She had never been so happy. Charles held her hands in his and could hardly speak.

Walking together in the late autumn sunshine that afternoon, they decided that their mutual affection for each other was too great to ignore, and that they should enjoy what happiness they could. Rachel asked, and Charles agreed, that they should start slowly, innocently and what's more, discreetly, with a series of meetings on Rachel's free half day. There were many English women parading freely around the city with the French officers, but Rachel did not want to upset her family, and she explained as much to Charles. Being considerate by nature, he understood immediately. He also realised that Rachel had little experience of men and that too sudden or too rough an approach would scare her away. He sensed her shyness and her insecurity and loved her for it. When she left him to return to the vicarage, he merely kissed her hand gently.

The sun was sinking in a blaze of glory as Rachel walked home. The dying rays glinted off the river Nene and dazzled her. She felt so happy that she didn't notice the black clouds of night gathering in the distance; but where there is light there must also be darkness.

Chapter 9

A couple of months passed, and Charles and Rachel were happy. They didn't make plans or talk about the future. They just enjoyed being together.

As autumn changed into winter, however, outdoor meetings became colder and more uncomfortable. They took to meeting in a country church away from the centre of the city, in Yaxley, near the prison camp, but it was far from ideal. They wished they could find somewhere warmer and more discreet, but it was difficult.

St Peter's church had several aisles and chapels off to the side, and the only place they could be safe from unwanted attention was in the darkest, furthest reaches of the west aisle. A churchwarden eyed them suspiciously as they entered that afternoon, making Rachel suddenly feel self-conscious. Somewhat naturally, Charles' bright coloured clothing attracted people's stares, and she was wary of being seen too close to him.

It's a shame, Rachel thought, for he was a striking looking man whom she would have been proud to be seen with; strong, tall, muscular with good features.

'If only we didn't have to hide,' she said. 'It's my fault, I know. I'm just trying not to hurt anyone's feelings.'

'My cherie,' replied Charles, 'I understand completely. Do not worry yourself.'

They strolled down the aisles and came across some wall paintings. One in particular caught Rachel's eye.

'How gruesome!' she declared, 'A grave digger and a skeleton! What were they thinking of when they painted it?'

Charles mused for a moment or two.

'We all end up there eventually,' he remarked thoughtfully. 'Maybe it is best to accept that.'

'Well, I don't like being reminded of it,' Rachel said. 'It makes me shudder to think about the end. I can't bear the thought of being nothing!'

'You will never be nothing,' Charles smiled. 'You belong with the angels, and they will enfold you in their wings when the day comes.'

'Oh please!' cried Rachel. 'Don't talk of that!'

'Pardon, my cherie. Let us walk on and forget these things.'

It was a dark and stormy day in late November when some dreadful news came, like a thief in the night, determined to steal their happiness. The wind was howling around the vicarage and the rain was lashing against the small leaded windows. In between sorting out the laundry and deciding on the next week's menus, Rachel gazed out and was surprised to see Elizabeth hurrying down the path. Instantly, Rachel knew something was wrong and she rushed to let her in at the servants' entrance. Her sister was bundled up against the cold in an old woollen shawl, covering her grey hair and surrounding her care worn face, but Rachel could see that she was very distressed.

'Rachel, dear sister – it's awful! I had to come and see you to tell you the terrible news. Edward has been killed in action, against those wicked Frenchmen! Sarah had a letter today. She is heartbroken. They were so close. And James is still missing – we've heard nothing in months!'

With that she burst into tears. 'They were so young!' she cried. 'How can this be?'

Rachel felt stunned, hardly knowing what to think or feel. Then all the memories came flooding back – Edward as a child: giving her wildflowers, playing games down by the river, struggling with his numbers, laughing with his sisters and brother, hugging her at bedtime. It was all so clear and yet now so painful. He'd been such a dear boy who had turned into a fine young man, handsome and strong. James too – what of him? Where was he? Was he still alive? Less sensitive than Eddie, but still a decent, caring person, already promised in marriage to a young local girl, who would dearly mourn his loss, if that was indeed the case. It must be awful not knowing, Rachel thought briefly, and resolved to go and see Becky, his intended. But the dreadful knowledge of Eddie's end was all too much for her to cope with at that moment, and she sank down onto a chair, grief like a heavy weight upon her shoulders. The boys had been as close to her as if they had been her own children, something she knew she would never have now.

Then an overwhelming feeling of guilt swept over her. What was she doing – consorting with the enemy? Charles was one of Eddie's killers! With this thought she started to sob bitterly, feeling angry with herself, with Charles and with the world in general, for allowing this to happen. Nothing made sense anymore.

A few days later Charles waited alone in the lonely church,

wondering where Rachel was. Maybe she'd had to work extra hours, he reasoned. She never missed their meetings normally. An hour passed and he sadly returned to the marketplace to make it look like he'd been there all afternoon. If it was found that he wasn't tending his stall whilst on parole, he could get into serious trouble. It would be the black hole for sure.

Halliday jeered at Charles when he returned to the prison camp that evening looking forlorn and dejected.

'What's up with you then, Frenchie? Sold none of yer trash, today then? Not surprising with that rubbish!'

The turnkey laughed mockingly and walked off, leaving Charles to fume quietly to himself.

The following Wednesday Charles was further concerned when Rachel did not do her usual shopping at the vegetable stall opposite. He did not know that Rachel had asked the maid Kitty to go in her place, feigning a headache.

The last week had found Rachel in an emotional turmoil. She was distressed and angry, and could not face seeing anyone French, let alone Charles. On the day she was supposed to be meeting him in Yaxley she had hidden herself away in her housekeeper's room and cried all afternoon. Polly could hear sobs as she came past the door, but upon knocking she was told firmly to: 'Go away!'

'Missus Alderman's in a right state,' she told Kitty. 'Cryin' fit to bust, she is, bless 'er.'

'Shame; wish we could help. I guess it's all over that young lad who got killed.'

'Told me to clear off, she did, but I understand. She don't want us to see 'er like that.'

Later that day Rachel apologised to the cook, blaming it all on her grief for her nephew, but it was more than that and she knew it. It was guilt and anger and regret.

There could be no funeral for dear Edward, his body lying in shattered pieces in a battlefield, far away. This was a further bitter pill to swallow. Rachel joined Sarah, Elizabeth and the rest of their family in a small church service of remembrance, but it was a pitiful affair – no coffin, no body, no grave. It made it hard to even believe it was true, except that Eddie's effects had been returned to them, along with a medal for services rendered.

Rachel saw her brother-in-law John again for the first time in many years and was shocked by how much he had aged. Walking with difficulty and leaning on his younger wife Ellen's arm for support, he looked like a broken man. They exchanged a few words, but it was awkward. Rachel reminded him too much of the past, and of his first wife, Mary. Rachel wished she could talk to him about it but it was not to be.

Two weeks went by, and Rachel had stayed away from all possibilities of meeting Charles. Half of her desperately wanted to find solace in his arms, but the other half of her couldn't face seeing him. She'd not even been to talk to Rose about it. The pain was just too raw to be able to share.

While she was absentmindedly sorting out the household bills one afternoon, she was horrified therefore when Kitty came rushing in to see her, exclaiming:

'Missus Alderman!'

(Housekeepers were always addressed as Mrs, even when they weren't married. It was tradition).

'There's one of them Frenchies lurking round down by the

gate. I told 'im to clear off, but he says he wants to speak to you. Shall I fetch an officer?'

Rachel was shocked – Charles here? Surely not!

'No, no,' she stammered. 'I'll go and sort it out. Don't worry.'

'You take care, Missus Alderman, them's a dangerous lot.'

Reassuring Kitty that she would be fine, Rachel gathered up her courage and went out. Charles stood there, looking both annoyed and concerned.

'Rachel,' he began, but she hushed him with a gesture of her hand and led him down to the tiny walled kitchen garden where they could not be seen. It was cold and damp underfoot and most of the plants were dead and barren. Only a few winter vegetables bravely struggled on. As she walked, Rachel's grey housekeepers skirt brushed against the ground and became wet and muddy, but she was too disturbed to notice.

An awkward silence ensued.

'What do you think you're doing, coming here?' she asked suddenly, angry at his impertinence.

'My cherie, I was worried about you. I think maybe you are ill, or something?'

'I cannot see you again,' Rachel said in a flat voice. 'Go away.'

'But why, cherie?'

'Don't call me that!' she snapped.

'Just tell me why,' he begged, 'surely I deserve that.'

Rachel sighed. He was right of course but she felt so angry with him. If she let go of her self-control, she knew it would all pour out in a torrent of emotion and recrimination.

'I can't,' she said. 'Just go away and forget me.'

'No!' exclaimed Charles, getting angry now. 'I will not do the going away! Not until you have told me why.' He paused. 'Has your family found out? Is that it?'

Rachel tried to leave but he held her arm.

'No! You will tell me.' he insisted.

A flash of rage filled Rachel's heart.

'Alright then – if you must know! Your dreadful countrymen have killed my dear nephew Edward, and I shall never forgive them! You are all murderers! How could you?'

'Is that it?' he cried. 'But we are at war! That's what happens. Men are forced to kill each other in order to survive. Can you not see that?'

She turned on him, eyes blazing.

'Have you killed, then?' she demanded.

Charles suddenly looked ashamed.

'Yes,' he said, sadly, 'I have, but only because I had to.'

'So, it could as easily have been you!' exclaimed Rachel. 'You could have killed Eddie, and you would have done!'

'Please,' pleaded Charles, 'please understand. If I don't kill my enemy, he will kill me. That is the horror of war. It is our duty.'

'Duty! Poor dear Eddie was hacked apart! How is that duty?'

'Listen Rachel, he would have done the same to me! I saw my own best friend cut down at my side by the English troops.

How is that fair? Both sides are the same. We have orders and we have to follow them. We have no choice.'

'Leave me alone!' cried Rachel. 'Go away. I never want to see you again!'

She turned to go but Charles grabbed her.

'No, Rachel, I will not. I cannot. Please!'

She fought him as he held her strongly, but gently, in his arms, hitting out at him and trying to push him away. But he held firm, and her struggles gradually subsided into sobs of bitter grief. Slowly the tears grew softer, and she allowed herself to be drawn in as he enfolded her with his arms, comforting and soothing her. Rachel leaned her head against his shoulder and found relief from her anger and pain there. She suddenly realised just how much she had come to depend on him.

It was the first time Charles had ever held Rachel in his arms like this and knowing her inexperience, he was careful not to scare her. He stroked her hair and kissed the top of her head as she leant against him, much as one would soothe a child. Then Rachel looked up at him, her eyes still sad but full of love. Seeing this, Charles gently kissed her properly on the lips for the first time and was happy to find that she responded willingly.

'I love you, my cherie,' Charles whispered. 'Don't leave me, I beg you.'

Hesitantly, Rachel stroked his face with her hand, gazing up at him.

'I love you, too,' she replied shyly, and they embraced once again.

Unbeknown to the couple at that moment, Kitty stood staring at them in shock, from the garden gate. She could hardly believe her eyes! Concerned for Rachel's safety with the unknown Frenchman, Kitty had finally decided she ought to go and check whether her supervisor was well. Having only been there a minute, she had not heard any of their previous conversation. Embarrassed and confused, Kitty turned and fled, questions racing through her head. What was going on? Had Rachel lost her mind? Should she tell Polly?

'What's up with you, lass?' asked Polly as Kitty came running in, looking flustered.

'Nothing, nothing,' she stammered and grabbing a duster as an excuse, disappeared off upstairs to think it through alone. Later she realised that she should have told Polly at the time, but now she couldn't find it in her heart to talk about it. If Missus Alderman was having an affair with a Frenchie – well that was up to her, she supposed, though it could only lead to trouble. These things were sure to end badly, in her opinion. Kitty was no gossip, however, and remembering how Rachel had helped her out in the past, she decided a policy of 'live and let live' was probably best. For the moment at least, their secret was safe.

Chapter 10

Next morning the storm had cleared away and the new day dawned cold and bright, the sun shining in a clear blue sky. Nevertheless, Rachel's heart was full of darkness. She knew now, without a doubt, that she loved Charles and that he loved her, but it frightened her. The intensity of yesterday's emotions had left her feeling afraid and all she wanted to do was run away from it. She no longer blamed Charles for Eddie's death; her anger and guilt were all spent. Yet she was in turmoil. Rachel was not naïve even though she was inexperienced in the ways of love, and she knew that this affair could easily become passionate, something that she needed to step back from. When she parted from Charles the day before she had been so happy, but night-time brought fear and insecurity like demons to taunt her. Now panic seized her in its grip.

Charles embraced Rachel warmly when they met at the church the following week, but he was surprised to find she shrank away from him.

'Charles, no,' she stammered, 'not here, please.'

'My cherie, what is wrong? Are you not happy?'

'I, I, well…' she began nervously, 'it's all too much, you see.'

'But you love me, no?' Charles asked anxiously, studying her face.

'Yes, it's true,' she replied, 'but I can't deal with it at the moment. It's all new to me.'

Charles looked sad. 'What can I do, my cherie? Tell me and I will try and help.'

'You're a good man,' Rachel told him, 'But I need some space. I feel so scared.'

'You do not need to be scared of me,' he said. 'I would never hurt you.'

'I am not scared of you,' she said. 'I am scared of myself, of my own feelings. I feel as if I am losing control and I don't like it.'

'Dearest – cherie – that is love. We have to face up to it or lose it. We have no choice.' He moved towards her, but she backed away.

'I must go, Charles. It's not your fault. I will see you next week when hopefully I will feel stronger. I'm sorry.'

With tears in her eyes Rachel ran out of the church into the winter rain and hurried home.

Charles did not attempt to follow her. He was sad but was trying to understand. In spite of her mature age, he knew she was still innocent and insecure. With time he hoped to gain her trust and win her love.

Meanwhile the more Rachel thought about it all, the more panic stricken she got, until she resolved that the best solution was to go and talk to the only other person who understood her – Rose.

Rachel was delighted to see Rose up and about when she visited her a couple of days later. True, she was leaning heavily on a stick and coughing frequently, but her eyes were bright and her voice clear. It had been a few weeks since Rachel had last seen her, due to the dreadful news about Eddie, and she'd been worried that Rose might have deteriorated further, so she was relieved to find her so well.

They sat by the tiny stove and chatted, Rachel telling Rose the sad news about her nephew. Rose was sympathetic, but her keen mind detected things that Rachel was reluctant to confide.

'So that must have been very difficult for you,' Rose said, 'with your Frenchman, I mean.'

'My Frenchman?' exclaimed Rachel, all of a fluster, 'he's not my Frenchman!'

'Isn't he?' said Rose, 'well I think you know what I mean, don't you?'

Rachel blushed deeply and felt herself going hot under the collar. For a moment she was lost for words. Rose came to the rescue by suggesting they make some tea, which gave Rachel a welcome respite. By the time the kettle had boiled she had made up her mind that she must divulge her innermost thoughts to Rose. After all, wasn't that what she had come here for?

Even so, she stared at her cup of tea for some time, trying to find the right words. Rose waited patiently.

At last, Rachel burst out: 'It was awful! I was so angry with Charles, but worse still with myself. I hated what I was doing, and I felt so guilty, but I took it all out on him. He didn't deserve it. I told him that I couldn't see him anymore.' She paused, remembering.

'But things have changed again now.' Rose commented. It wasn't a question but a statement.

'How? How did you know?' Rachel gasped in surprise. 'Well, yes, they have.'

Rose smiled. 'I can see it in your face, my dear. You are in love.'

'It's true,' Rachel confessed. 'In fact, this has made us closer than ever. I don't know why it should.'

'Dark times can bring people together,' said Rose.

'Even when we are enemies?' asked Rachel.

'Yes dear, even then. The heart doesn't know any borders.'

They drank their tea, reflecting quietly on the vagaries of love.

'Are you happy?' Rose asked suddenly.

'No!' exclaimed Rachel. 'Oh, but I am as well! Oh, I don't know!'

'Tell me about it,' coaxed Rose. 'I can see you are troubled.'

'It's just - it's so intense - it scares me. I don't know how to handle it.' Her voice sank to a whisper. 'I just want to run away.'

Rose considered for a moment.

'Maybe you should just try and slow down a bit, give yourself some time to get used to things. Is this man rushing you?'

'No, he's not like that,' answered Rachel. 'He's been very patient. I'm so unused to men, but he's been very understanding.'

'So can't you tell him then, how you feel?'

'Well, yes, maybe, but it's so difficult. We get so little time to see each other and now the weather has turned bad, we can't meet outside anymore. We've been going to a little church out in Yaxley, but I'm sure the churchwarden is suspicious of us. He followed us around last time. We daren't meet in public. If my family find out, I'm sure they will never speak to me again.'

'Why don't you come here?' Rose suggested. 'I could stay upstairs in the bedroom, out of the way, which means you would have a chaperone, so to speak, and you wouldn't be alone. You would feel more confident then, I'm sure. I'd be around if you needed me. What's more, this place isn't much but at least it's warm and dry, and quite discreet. You'd be very welcome.'

Rachel stared at her in surprise.

'Really? Rose, that's a brilliant idea! Are you sure you don't mind?'

Rose patted her hand.

'Anything for you my dear,' she replied.

The almshouses were very small; a simple row of stone cottages, each with their own front door, in a quiet area of town. They only had two rooms – a bedroom upstairs and a living room downstairs. There was no proper kitchen, though basic food and drink could be prepared on the stove which also served to heat the place. Most food was brought in by local benefactors but like all charity, it could be hit and miss at times. Toilet facilities were outside and shared with all the other occupants. For those unable to reach them, due to age or frailty, chamber pots were also provided. Rose considered herself very lucky to have such a home. If she hadn't been offered one, she could have easily been out on the streets, begging. Without a family to care for you, there were few other options when you became elderly or sick.

Charles approached Rachel hesitantly at their next meeting but was pleased to see that she was smiling. She took his arm, and they promenaded down the aisle of the church.

'I have an idea,' she began, 'my friend Rose has offered us a place to meet indoors at her house. She will stay out of the way so we can talk, and it will be warmer than here.'

'Most places are!' joked Charles, as he saw his breath come out steaming in the freezing air.

'I know it means we won't be quite alone,' Rachel continued, 'but I think this will help me. My dear Charles, I am so sorry about last time, but I still feel so frightened of love and …', she faltered, 'and of what comes next.' She blushed deeply.

'Is that what is worrying you?' Charles asked, relieved. 'We do not have to pursue that, my darling. It is enough to be with you. I ask nothing more.'

'Maybe not,' she said looking embarrassed, 'but it might still happen.'

Charles smiled. 'Maybe, perhaps? Who knows, my cherie, but do not worry yourself.'

He paused.

'Anyway, I feel your idea is a good one and will be better for us. Thank your dear friend and tell her we will be glad to take up her offer. It's got to be better than here, to be sure!'

Charles felt a bit embarrassed when he turned up at Rose's house the following week. He didn't quite know what to expect when she opened the door.

'Madame, excuse me, I am Charles Le Boucher, and I am here for the meeting with Mam'selle Rachel.'

He needn't have worried however for Rose welcomed him warmly and took him into the parlour where Rachel was already waiting for him. Rose then left them alone together, retreating to her upstairs bedroom, but not before Charles had charmed her by presenting her with one of his hand carved trinkets, a tiny dolls house, shaped just like the alms-house itself.

'To thank you for your kindness, Madame,' he said, bowing. 'I hope it will bring pleasure.'

Rose thanked him profusely, blushing like a young girl, then took herself off upstairs.

There was a moment of awkwardness between them after this, then Charles burst out laughing.

'Well, my cherie, what a thing this is! We are quite the mystery couple are we not?'

Rachel laughed too and the awkwardness vanished like a puff of smoke in the breeze. Their natural intimacy resumed, but in a way that helped Rachel's confidence. Knowing Rose was just upstairs made her feel protected and safe. They talked, laughed and even occasionally kissed, but Charles was gentle and loving. When they finally returned that afternoon to their respective abodes, they both felt happy and relaxed. Life, thought Rachel, was getting better again.

Chapter 11

Meanwhile things were slowly changing at the vicarage. Reverend Tutte's widowed sister Mrs Green had finally cast off her widow's weeds some time before and started wearing elegant but subdued outfits in hues of blue, grey and brown. Recently however, she could often be seen in clouds of frothy lace and silk in pastel shades.

'A sure sign,' Polly remarked to Kitty, 'that the Mistress is in love.'

'Never!' said Kitty. 'Surely not.'

But it appeared to be true, for gentlemen visitors came and went regularly. Matters eventually resolved themselves into one particular visitor – a smartly dressed British officer, with scarlet uniform and handlebar moustache. Mrs Letitia Green simpered and blushed whenever he was near, and the servants took much amusement in discussing her affairs of the heart.

'Behaving like a giddy young girl again, she is,' remarked Polly.

Kitty agreed laughing. 'I saw her fluttering her fan at him yesterday. Really! At her age, I don't know!'

Rachel didn't join in the gossip much and hadn't really taken a great deal of notice, being somewhat preoccupied with her own 'affair of the heart.' Still, one morning things came to all their attention with an announcement.

To their great surprise all the staff were called up unexpectedly to see the Reverend in his drawing room. There was a frantic dash around from all of them to tidy themselves up for this unusual attention and then they trotted upstairs. Kitty worried constantly.

'Do you think they's getting rid of us all? Perhaps they's moving house and don't need us no more.'

'Kitty!' admonished Rachel. 'Don't speculate. The master will tell us soon enough.'

Luckily for them, however, it was happier news. Mrs Green was betrothed to Major Holland and the wedding was set to be in mid-January, just after the Christmas season. The happy couple would then be setting up home in central London. The servants offered the merry widow their heartiest congratulations and prepared to depart, but there was more.

The Reverend spoke:

'As my dear sister is soon to leave us, I would like to give a party at Christmas time for all our family and friends. I know we usually spend the time in quiet meditation on the holiness of the season, but I feel this special occasion warrants something different.'

Christmas was indeed a sombre affair at the vicarage, normally. The Reverend worked in the cathedral throughout most of it and, apart from an excess of good food, things carried on much as usual in the household. Even though Christmas Day was officially a holiday for most people, servants such as themselves still worked right through looking after their household's needs, in the hope of maybe a Christmas box on St Stephen's Day. The Reverend did not forget his obligations in this respect, but the gifts were not over generous, merely a small token of his appreciation. He didn't believe in frivolities at any time, let alone Christmas, which he sincerely believed should be purely devoted to Christian worship. Mrs Green, in her turn, usually gave them a small gift of fruit and nuts as was traditional for the poor.

'Big of 'er!' Polly exclaimed the first time. 'I'm surprised she can spare it really!'

'How the other half live!' said Kitty, wistfully.

Rachel smiled quietly but didn't comment.

As they made their way back down below stairs, Polly started to grumble.

'Loads of extra work and no thanks, mind. Just got to get on with it, no help.'

Rachel tried to pacify her.

'I'll talk to the mistress and try and get someone extra in for the occasion.'

'Well, that'd be more like it,' conceded Polly. 'I mean to say, how we expected to cope otherwise, just the three of us?'

'We can all chip in together,' piped up Kitty, but Polly gave her a withering look.

'Don't be silly, girl. Who's gonna peel all the taters? You? And what about drinks? We'll need a butler or sommat.'

'I'll see what I can do,' promised Rachel, ever the peacemaker and the organiser.

True to her word Rachel made an appointment to see Mistress Green the next day. As a servant one couldn't just turn up and expected to be admitted, unless called for. Even a housekeeper was supposed to be as invisible as possible.

'Well?' asked Mrs Green, 'What is it? I'm very busy, you know.'

Busy? thought Rachel privately, busy doing what? She doesn't know the meaning of the word. Instead, she just murmured demurely, 'Yes of course Madam, I quite understand.' (She had always found that this approach had the best effect on the highly strung lady).

Mrs Green calmed down and Rachel was able to talk to her about the party.

'How many guests are there to be, Madam?'

'About fifty, I should think.'

'Will it be a full dinner party?'

'Yes of course.'

'Well Madam, we were wondering if we could have some extra help for the occasion.'

'Extra! That will cost a lot. You three should be able to manage.'

'Oh yes, Madam, I'm sure we shall, but you see we will need someone to greet people and serve drinks, if we are to do this well. We also need extra help with the vegetable preparation. I'm sure you wouldn't want it to look shoddy.'

'No, no, of course not. This is very important to me. It is our engagement party.'

'All the more reason to make a special effort. These things need to be done properly, don't you agree, Madam?'

By the end of the conversation Rachel had talked the Mistress into hiring a footman, a butler and a kitchen maid for the event. She smiled to herself as she left the room. The Mistress was quite easy to persuade really, if you knew the right way. If only the rest of life was as simple as this.

Preparations for the party went on apace. Food was ordered, staff hired, the parsonage cleaned from top to bottom. They were all quite exhausted before it even started. There was even to be dancing and a string quartet was found to provide the music.

'How exciting!' said Kitty, her eyes shining. 'Nothing like this happens normally.'

Perhaps the Mistress should get engaged more often!' remarked Polly, wryly.

Rachel laughed but was finding it all a strain. She'd hardly had a day off in the last few weeks and had only seen dear Charles very briefly. She missed him, but at least he knew the reason and understood. She wondered what Christmas would be like for him in the prison camp. When she asked him about it, he told her 'It's mostly lots of prayers and hymns, but none of our own, just English ones.'

'Do you get any extra food?' Rachel asked.

'Not really,' he replied, 'sometimes some fruit from the townspeople's guild.'

On the last day she saw Charles before Christmas, Rachel gave him a small present that she had made herself – a pair of knitted gloves. Charles was truly touched.

'You are so thoughtful,' he murmured in her ear, holding her close. 'But see, I have something for you, also.'

He produced a tiny carving of a house.

'It's delightful,' Rachel said, 'I wish it was ours and we could live there happily ever after.'

Charles' face clouded over.

'I fear it cannot be, my sweet, but it is a lovely thought.'

They held each other tight, wrapped in their own dreams, longing to stay together forever. The wrench of parting got worse each time now.

By the time Christmas and the highly anticipated party had finished, Rachel was shattered. The constant work had drained all her strength, so much so that a bad cold finally confined her to bed for a couple of days. Kitty brought her broth and hot drinks, and she recovered enough to visit her family at New Year. Rachel saw very little of them these days; after all she was the only one unmarried and working in service. Her older brothers continued to prosper in their businesses, and sister Elizabeth had a large family now. Furthermore, things were awkward with niece Sarah now, since Eddie's sad demise and James' disappearance. Rachel hardly knew what to say.

'We never see you anymore,' complained Sarah. 'You used to visit on your days off, but now you don't. Are you so busy all the time?'

Rachel felt guilty remembering all the time that she now spent with Charles. She blushed and stammered.

'Yes, yes, very busy at the vicarage. Hardly a moment to myself.'

'You must take some time for yourself, Aunty. Tell them you need to have some time off. Maybe I should speak to them about it.'

'No!' said Rachel, alarmed. 'Please don't. That would be embarrassing.'

'Yes, well I don't think it's fair, anyway. Now let's go and see the children.'

Rachel breathed a sigh of relief. The last thing she wanted was for Sarah to find out that she did get time off, but that she spent it elsewhere. She made a mental note to try and see more of her family. Then she felt guilty all over again.

The party had been a great success and Rachel had been much complimented on her smooth handling of it, by the Reverend and his sister. Just after New Year she received a summons to attend the mistress upstairs in the parlour. What now? she thought.

Mrs Green smiled as Rachel came in, and then, quite unexpectedly, invited her to sit down on a chair. This made her feel very awkward. It wasn't her place.

'Oh no, Ma'am. I'm not sure I should.'

'Please, I'd like to talk to you.'

Rachel perched uneasily on the edge of a plush armchair, feeling uncomfortable.

'I would like to thank you for all your hard work in arranging my engagement party,' began the widow.

'It was my pleasure, Ma'am,' murmured Rachel.

'Well, I have a further task for you, if you will consent. As you know, after the wedding, I will be moving to London and I would like you to set up the house there for me – engage servants, organise deliveries, stock the larder and so on. I need someone I can trust. If you wanted to, you could even stay on permanently. It's in a very good part of London. My brother has agreed to the idea as long as you are happy about it.'

Rachel could scarcely believe what she was hearing. London! She'd heard so much about it and had always wanted to go there, but her heart belonged here, now. She sat there, stunned, trying to take it all in. Finally, she said:

'Oh no, Ma'am. I couldn't move there permanently. I have family here, you see.'

'Of course. I understand. So, shall we say you will come for two weeks then, to get everything in place? I'll make all the travel arrangements. You will be leaving on the day after our wedding on the 21st of January. We are away on honeymoon for a fortnight so you will have a free hand to do whatever is needed.'

Rachel nodded. How had she been talked into this? She left the room, her thoughts in a whirl. Two weeks! Two weeks in London, the city that she had heard so much about. How exciting! Then again, how scary! All at once Rachel thought: I can't do this! It's too much. I won't be able to cope. I'll have to resign. You're a failure, Rachel, she told herself, and you won't be able to pull this off. Everyone will find out what a fraud you are. They think you're really good at your job, but it's all a bluff. She sighed. I don't have what it takes to run a London household – and yet – and yet – I wish I could.

A couple of days later Rachel got a well-deserved day off so she decided to go and see Charles. By that time however, she had worked herself into a state of utter panic about the proposed London trip. She couldn't sleep, she could hardly eat; fear just paralysed her.

Kitty remarked to Polly:

'Missus Alderman's in a bad way, don't you think? Perhaps she's sickening for something.'

'Mebbee,' replied the cook. 'Sommat's up with 'er that's for sure.'

The two servants liked and respected Rachel, but they certainly didn't understand her moods. She was a locked door to them, beyond which they couldn't pass. Only two people in the world truly knew her, and they were Rose and Charles. It was to them she went now to pour out her troubles.

As soon as Rachel caught sight of them both standing in the doorway of Rose's cottage, she burst into tears.

'My cherie, what is wrong?' asked Charles, his arms around her already.

Looking concerned, Rose guided her in to sit down. Between them they heard Rachel's outpouring of panic and fear about her forthcoming task.

'I can't do it! I know I can't,' she exclaimed between sobs. 'I'm not up to it!'

Charles held her tight whilst Rose made them some tea.

'Calm down, my petite,' he said. 'You are very, how do you say it, capable. You must believe in yourself more.'

Rose agreed. 'Dear Rachel, you are very good at your job, I know, I've seen you do it. You're efficient and organised. Of course, you can do it. That's why the mistress asked you. It's a compliment.'

'I know,' sobbed Rachel, 'but London – it's so different to

being here.'

Charles smiled gently. 'Not so very different, I am thinking. Busier perhaps, and noisier, but otherwise not so different really.'

'But there will be lots more servants to organise, and the house will be much grander. I won't know what to do.'

'Look,' said Rose, 'I've been in a big house or two in my time. I can tell you all the information you need to know. Don't worry!'

'Really?' said Rachel sounding happier, 'that would be such a help. But then …' (and she gazed at Charles) .. 'I will be away from you all for a few weeks and I will miss you both so much.'

Charles kissed her forehead and held her hand.

'A couple of weeks, that's all. It's not so very long. And think of all the wonderful things you will see in London. You must take this chance, my cherie, it will be so good for you.'

'We will both miss you,' said Rose, 'but Charles is right. You will enjoy it once you get there.'

'It is so far away,' Rachel said but in spite of this, she was beginning to think more positively about the opportunity. By the time they parted she had made up her mind that she would give it her best shot. She would not let this defeat her.

Chapter 12

Sitting in the stagecoach on the way to London, Rachel felt nervous. She had never travelled in one before and the shaking of the coach due to the rutted and uneven track, made her feel quite ill. The woodwork inside was rough and splintered, and her clothes were soon caught and torn by it as she was tossed around. Not only that but she had heard a great deal about the vagabonds that preyed on unwary travellers and often laid in wait for the stagecoach to pass by. So it was with some relief that she alighted after two days and countless changeovers of horses, stiff and weary, but all in one piece.

London was dirtier and noisier than she could have ever imagined after rural Peterborough. Despite this, as the stagecoach came in through the turnpike gate at Hyde Park Corner, Rachel was amazed to see the large green expanse of the park amidst all the city grime. A short ride in a hansom cab to the house she was to work in for the next couple of weeks, took her past many fine buildings such as Buckingham House, the Abbey and the Palace of Westminster. She made a mental note to visit them properly whilst she was here. Peterborough had no buildings as fine or large as these, though the cathedral was impressive enough in its own way.

The newlywed's house was in a smart suburb of Westminster, in a quiet cul de sac. When Rachel first caught sight of it, she had to catch her breath. It was fine and stately, though in actual fact, not as grand as those of the truly wealthy. The captain and his new bride were not aristocracy after all, merely well to do upper class, but compared to the middle-class vicarage, this was indeed a step up.

Most of the staff were due to start the following week, but Rachel was greeted with the utmost respect by the butler, Mr Johnson.

'We are most pleased to have you here, Mrs Alderman,' he said warmly. 'The new Mistress has been most fulsome in your praise.'

'Really?' said Rachel, surprised.

'Of course,' he replied. 'With all your experience of running a household successfully, how could she not be?'

Rachel felt an inner glow of satisfaction. Too few people had appreciated her in life, and this was something new to her. She determined to do the best she possibly could for the household. To this end, she set about ordering supplies, arranging drapes and furnishings, interviewing and advising staff and generally setting up the new abode. Johnson was most impressed.

The two weeks whizzed by, and Rachel had to admit she'd enjoyed it. In the little time she'd had free she had found the confidence to visit some of London's attractions, though she was careful not to travel on foot. The city was a dangerous place for anyone, especially a solitary woman. Her thoughts, however, turned often to Charles and she wished she could have shared it all with him. This could never be, she knew, and she regretted it deeply.

In the last couple of days before leaving for home, Rachel had one last important job to do – engage a housekeeper to take over from herself on a permanent basis. Johnson had shortlisted several prospective candidates and Rachel had interviewed them all, but somehow, they didn't seem to fit.

Trying to decide between the most likely two she decided to take herself for a walk in the nearby park. It was a sunny afternoon and she stayed well in view of other people at all times. Sitting down on a bench she reflected on the post. It needed someone firm but fair, perhaps someone who needed a challenge and a new opportunity. Lost in reverie her thoughts were interrupted by a well-dressed, middle-aged woman politely asking if she could share the seat.

'Of course,' Rachel replied, gladly giving way. Within a few minutes she found herself chatting to the unknown woman as strangers often do, never thinking that they might meet again.

'London is such a large and noisy place,' remarked Rachel. 'I'm not used to it. Are you?'

The woman smiled. 'I grew up here,' she said, 'and was married in St Bartholomew's Church, in Smithfield, near the Elms.'

'The Elms – what's that?' asked Rachel. 'Is it a woodland?'

The woman laughed. 'No, my dear. Sad to say, it was a place of execution for rogues, long ago!'

'Really?' Rachel shuddered. 'How awful! What did they do to them?'

'Oh, the usual, you know. Sometimes burned, they say, sometimes hanged, drawn and quartered. Still, it's not done there now. T'was a long time ago.'

Rachel felt a revulsion for such terrible deeds. No matter what anyone had done, she could not find it in her heart to wish that on them.

'Well of course, hanging is still a common enough punishment these days. Pity the poor wretches.'

'Yes, indeed,' sighed Rachel.

To change the subject, she asked the woman about herself.

'My husband unfortunately died of the flux last year,' she told her, 'So I'm all alone now and looking for work. We've got a daughter but thankfully she's married a nice young man and is settled. I just need to earn me keep now, you know, but it's tricky to find someone to take you on with no references. And to think I ran me own household for twenty years – you'd think that would count for something!'

'You know,' said Rachel thoughtfully, 'you could be just the person I'm looking for.'

By the end of the afternoon Rachel had engaged Mrs Bennett on a trial basis for the Hollands. She felt quite content with her impulsive decision, but it did mean that she would have to stay an extra week to make sure all was well. Aware that Charles would be eagerly awaiting her return, Rachel felt torn between her emotions and her duty, but duty had to come first unfortunately and so she stayed on.

Charles meanwhile dreamed of her, pined for her, and longed for her return. His usual tormenter, Halliday, was as cruel and heartless as ever, but with Rachel around Charles could usually rise above it. Not this time. When Rachel failed to appear after the promised two weeks Charles' reactions to the warder's provocations landed him in the black hole again. A week later, dazed and half starved, he was finally allowed out into the daylight. Staggering out he was brutally knocked to his feet by Halliday.

'Down there, where you belong, you dog!' he snarled, and

Charles grovelled in the dirt, too weak to do anything else. The warder laughed and walked away. Johannes, a cheerful Dutch man who was friends with Charles, helped him up and gave him water, which revived him. In spite of the initial language difficulties Johannes and Charles had made an instant connection. Johannes had a pretty, young wife and a 4-year-old son with him as well, and nothing seemed to trouble him. Charles envied him at times.

'Take care, my friend,' the Dutch man warned him now. 'You know Halliday would love to send you to the hulks, if he could.'

(The hulks were a terrifying prospect – derelict ships moored off the coast, used to hold as many convicts as they could squeeze in. Conditions were rumoured to be inhuman).

'I know,' replied Charles, 'but he just gets to me, every time.'

'If only Rachel would come back,' he thought to himself. 'I need her so much.'

But another visit to Rose's house a couple of days later brought no news and no sign of his beloved.

Desperate, Charles made up his mind to call on the vicarage and see if Rachel had returned. So, after packing up his market stall early the next day he headed there. Gazing at the solidly respectable middle-class dwelling, Charles felt suddenly self-conscious in his brightly coloured prison uniform. How could he call and ask for her? True, he had been there once before, but it had not been an easy experience. Eventually he made up his mind and worked his way round to the kitchen door. His knock was timid. Polly opened the door expecting a delivery of coal. She looked at him suspiciously.

'You ain't the coalman!' she said, stating the obvious. 'What you want?'

Charles eyed the generously proportioned cook nervously.

'I, er, that is, Madame, per'aps you will allow me to see Mam'selle Rachel?'

'There ain't no-one 'ere of that name. Don't know what you're talking about!'

Charles suddenly realised that Polly would only know his dearest as 'Mrs Alderman' and he stammered:

'I mean Madame Alderman – the keeper of the house.'

'Why do you want 'er? She don't talk to you lot, you know. 'Er nephew was killed by one of you. You better clear off!'

Just at that moment, Kitty arrived at the door to see what all the fuss was about.

'I recognise him, Polly,' she said. 'He's been 'ere to see the Missus before.'

Kitty looked him in the eye, remembering privately what she had seen on that occasion. For a moment she almost pitied him. He looked so obviously distressed.

'What do you want?' she asked, not unkindly.

'Please, I just want to know if she is here.'

'Well, she ain't,' retorted Polly, 'not that it's any business of yours! What's more we don't know when she will be back – maybe never! So, get lost, Frenchie!'

Charles hung his head and retreated sadly. Still no Rachel – but at least he knew she hadn't returned yet. He had faith that she would come back to him soon. For now, he just had to be patient.

The week's trial was going well but Rachel hesitated to leave. There was still so much to tell her replacement. More time went by than she intended, and Rachel was beginning to feel desperate. She knew she loved Charles beyond all doubt, and she missed him so much. Somehow, she had to get away to go home.

Finally on a cold and wet Sunday in February, Rachel was able to embark on the arduous stagecoach journey back to Peterborough. On the way back, all she could think about was seeing Charles again, and mentally she tried to urge the coach to go as quickly as possible. The weather, however, was very poor and the trip was an exceptionally slow one. At one point the coach got so bogged down in mud that everyone had to get out and wait in a nearby cottage for several hours, whilst the coachman and horses fought their way out of it. Rachel's frustration at the delay was almost overwhelming. How could they be taking so long?

It was a relief when, somewhat later than planned, they eventually reached their destination and Rachel caught sight of the familiar spires of Peterborough Cathedral. Home at last!

The next day after a brief catch up with the staff, Rachel made a hasty excuse to go into town.

'Really,' she said. 'I don't know what you've been doing whilst I've been away. We seem to have run out of everything!'

Polly and Kitty weren't best pleased by these remarks, but as Kitty pointed out:

'It ain't our place to argue none. She's in charge, after all.'

'Hmm,' replied Polly. 'Mebbee she's just tired out from all the travelling. It ain't like her really.'

Rachel rushed through all her errands, giving out orders for deliveries to be made direct to the vicarage, not waiting to collect the goods. Then she practically ran all the way to Rose's cottage. What if he wasn't there? Maybe he was tired of waiting for her? Her heart was pounding as she reached the door but there was Charles, beaming, ready to enfold her in his arms. There was a long passionate embrace, which Rose studiously avoided by making tea on the tiny stove.

'My cherie, my darling,' Charles cried. 'I have missed you so much. You are my only love. Never go away again. I cannot stand it!' He stroked her hair and kissed her again.

Rachel gazed at him, studying every line of his face.

'Dearest, dearest Charles. I don't want anyone else, and I will never leave you. I know now that we belong together, no matter what.'

There was a long loving silence, then Charles revealed:

'It is so strange. Before the war I was in prison with my marriage. Now that I am actually *in* a prison, I feel free! You are my angel. You give me wings and let me fly.'

'And you are my strength, my rock,' replied Rachel. 'Everything I have achieved is because of you. You make me strong.'

The tea was a long time coming as they had a lot to say, and Rose didn't care to interrupt them. At last, they all sat down together, and Rachel told them about her trip. Then she finished – 'I didn't know whether you would be here Charles, or whether you would have gone somewhere else.'

'He's been here every day for the last week,' Rose told her, smiling, though her face seemed more lined than Rachel remembered. 'Poor dear man, waiting so patiently for you to return.'

'It's true,' Charles admitted. 'I did not know what else to do. I tried visiting the vicarage, but they sent me away.'

'You poor thing,' Rachel sympathised. 'But all is well now. We are together again.'

'That is all that matters,' said Charles and they embraced again.

Chapter 13

It was the beginning of March and there was a touch of early spring in the air. With the better weather, Charles and Rachel had decided to take a stroll down by a discreet part of the river Nene, for a change. Few people came that way and the ones that did were clearly secret lovers. French officers and local girls, high class women and red coated soldiers – they were all there, trying not to be seen, just like Charles and Rachel. Even so, Rachel felt afraid that at any moment she might bump into someone she knew. It made her jittery, but Charles, as always, made her laugh with his tales of prison life. He told her stories of the lessons that the prison thrust upon them. Some like learning the English language had proved to be most useful, but others like reading plays or dancing, he just saw as absurd.

'Dancing,' he said. 'What use is that in a prison? Our countrymen already know the Cotillon anyway – it is French after all. The only people we can dance with are each other. Imagine, my cherie – grown men – soldiers - prancing around with each other as partners! My friend Johannes, he just treads on my feet the whole time!'

Rachel laughed, picturing the scene. It was only a week later however that Charles brought up the subject again and this time it was different.

'Cherie', he said, 'I have exciting news. The prison is holding a dance (to improve our minds, I think!). But they want ladies to come in and be our partners.'

Rachel stared at him, trying to take it all in. 'Partners?' she said.

'Yes, it means you could come into the prison and dance with me for an evening. Wouldn't that be wonderful?'

She could hardly believe her ears. Surely not! Why would the authorities want that? But indeed, it appeared they did. An inspection of the camp was due, and the governor wanted to make sure that the POWs were seen to be treated well.

'I'll get you a ticket, though you'll have to be vetted and searched, unfortunately. There were some problems before when people came in to watch a play, so they have tightened up security now.' He paused. 'You will come, my cherie, won't you?' he asked pleadingly. 'Please.'

'Of course,' agreed Rachel, her eyes shining with joy. 'I've never been to a dance before. My mother taught me years ago, but I've never had the chance to try it out for real. Oh Charles, this is wonderful! And a whole evening with you – what could be better?'

Charles smiled. 'I am glad you are pleased, my cherie, though I wish it were in a different place.'

'At least I'll get to see where you live,' said Rachel.

'I doubt you will see much of it,' replied Charles. 'The public will only see what the authorities want you to see.' His face clouded over. 'You won't see my hammock, upstairs in the barracks, crammed in with 100 other hammocks, or the black hole.' He shivered suddenly.

'My dearest,' said Rachel sympathetically, moving close to him and stroking his cheek. 'Let us think only of this lovely chance that we have. Try to forget the bad times.'

Charles had revealed enough of his experiences in the prison camp for her to understand his pain. Still, he had been careful to spare her the worst of it, especially his ongoing persecution by Halliday.

Rachel was excited by the thought of the forthcoming ball, and, like many a woman before her, her thoughts turned suddenly to what she should wear for the occasion. She had no dresses suitable for dancing. Most of her life was spent in her drab housekeeper's uniform of grey silk, with its old-fashioned full skirts and starched apron. The few other dresses she owned were also outdated, she realised, being mostly 'hand me downs' from Sarah and Elizabeth. The new straighter simpler lines of gowns had come in recently, but Rachel had never needed them. Now she decided, she had to get something new.

In spite of her excitement, Rachel spent some time gazing in the shop window of the dress shop before finally plucking up the courage to enter. The shop was small and quite dark but even so Rachel could see items of the most delicate muslin floating in the air. Her spirits rose. Pastel shades danced in front of her eyes. Simplicity and elegance were all the fashion now; dresses sleek and understated with high waists, straight skirts and puff sleeves like mini clouds. Rachel gazed in awe not knowing where to start. A smartly dressed young sales lady swooped in to offer her assistance.

'Can I help you, Madam?' she asked. 'We have all the latest styles straight from London. But if you would prefer a more traditional style for the older lady then this rail here may be more to your taste.'

She indicated a section of old style full skirted dresses.

'No, no, thank you,' replied Rachel. 'I'm going to a dance, and I want one of these. I'm just not sure which.'

At that point a figure moved out of the shadows who Rachel hadn't noticed before. Shocked, she recognised her niece Sarah – the last person she wanted to see right then.

'Aunty – How are you? I haven't seen you in ages. Going to a dance? How wonderful – where?'

Rachel knew that she daren't tell Sarah the truth. She would never have understood. Her mind raced to think of some excuse. She felt herself going bright red (something she hadn't done for a while) and she started to stammer.

'Oh, oh – the vicarage. That is, there's a dance there and I have to dress for it. I've been invited.'

'Really? That's unusual, isn't it?'

'It's a celebration,' lied Rachel desperately, 'all to do with the return of the Reverend's sister from her honeymoon.'

'Oh well! Aren't you lucky? What are you going to get?'

Crisis averted, Rachel and Sarah then spent a happy afternoon choosing her a beautiful diaphanous gown, along with gloves, shoes and even an ornament for her hair. The dress was of palest green – a shade which suited Rachel well. Wearing it made her feel special and she was floating on a cloud of happiness by the time she arrived home. Her parcel was safely tucked under her arm so that no-one should see, but she was unable to get past the eagle-eyed Polly, without comment being passed.

'Been shopping, then Mrs Alderman? Got yerself something pretty to wear, 'ave you? Good fer you. We all needs a few treats now and then.'

Rachel fled to the privacy of her housekeeper's room, her

cheeks scarlet with embarrassment. Nevertheless, that night she couldn't resist taking out the beautiful item and letting it hang where she could see and admire it. She thought she had never seen anything so lovely.

On the evening of the ball Rachel dressed with special care, even attempting to put her hair up for the occasion. This was something she rarely did, and so she started to struggle. It seemed that every time she got one bit under control, another part would become wayward. Time was slipping by, and Rachel was getting frustrated. Would she ever get this right? Just then Rachel heard Kitty come past her door and she impulsively called out to her, and practically dragged her in.

'Kitty please – you've got to help me! My hair – I can't do it. Please!'

Rachel was nearly in tears. She wanted so badly for everything to be perfect.

'Mrs Alderman – you look lovely if you don't mind me saying. What's wrong? Your hair? Oh, don't worry, I can have that fixed in a jiffy.'

Within a few minutes Kitty's nimble fingers had fashioned Rachel's disobedient locks into an attractive style. The addition of the hair ornament completed the effect and Rachel was ready. She could hardly recognise herself in the mirror. True, she would never be 'beautiful' in the classic meaning of the word, but she had made the best of her features. What's more she positively glowed from within with happiness.

'Where you going, Mrs Alderman?' asked Kitty, admiring her.

'I, er, well, I can't really say, but it's a dance.'

Kitty smiled. She kept a keen ear open for the local gossip and had heard about a certain event on up at the prison depot tonight. She said nothing however, except:

'Well, have a lovely time. Enjoy yourself. You deserve it.'

There was a queue of young ladies waiting outside the prison gates when Rachel reached there. She was among the oldest of them she realised, but tonight she didn't care. All she wanted was to be with Charles, to dance, to live for a while in a different way and create beautiful memories. She was a little daunted by the thick prison walls, the grim-faced warders and the guns that seemed to be everywhere, but her excitement soon overcame her fears. Submitting to the embarrassment of a body search, she kept her mind firmly on the prospect ahead. At the entrance to the dance hall a particularly sour faced warden growled:

'Name?'

'Rachel Alderman,' she responded timidly.

He checked her off his list and enquired gruffly: 'Have you an allocated partner for this evening, Ma'am?'

'Charles Le Boucher,' she replied, feeling proud.

The warden sneered.

'Him? Oh well, best of luck with that rogue! I didn't even know he could dance.'

Halliday, for it was him, snorted derisively and turned to the next lady in the queue. Rachel felt annoyed – how dare he talk about Charles like that? But as she entered the hall, she forgot all about it and her spirits soared.

For one night only the prisoners had been allowed to wear their soldiers' uniforms again if they still had them. (Some men of course had lost them through gambling). Many of these were ragged now but the men had done their best to repair and restore them to their former glory. Rachel was amazed to see Charles, resplendent in dark blue, looking so smart and handsome. He came towards her, smiling, holding out both hands.

'Cherie, my love, you are so beautiful. It's as if I am seeing you again for the first time.'

They embraced, but a swift order from a nearby guard meant that they had to separate.

'No fraternising with the guests! They are only here to dance with you, for your education.'

Charles led Rachel to the dance floor where they spent a pleasant hour dancing the English country dance. Lines were formed and they had to dance up and down them. It was a lively pace and Rachel skipped along as best she could. It was wonderful to be here, spending the evening with her love.

At the interval the prisoners fetched refreshments for their partners, and they were able to sit down and talk for a while.

'My feet are sore!' laughed Rachel. 'I didn't know it would be so tiring. I've never danced before.'

'You can't tell,' said Charles. 'You are a dancer naturelle.'

After a rest, Charles was able to lead her away from the throng into a quiet alcove where they sat in delicious closeness, quiet and happy.

'I wish things could always be like this,' Rachel said wistfully.

Charles kissed her forehead.

'We have tonight,' he said. 'Let's enjoy what we can.'

The second half began with the Cotillon and then later the Scotch Reel, though both Rachel and Charles struggled with that one. They ended up getting in a tangle, laughing as they tried to avoid wrecking the whole thing. Out of breath they collapsed onto chairs at the side of the room, to sit the last one out.

'I can hardly bear to leave,' said Rachel. 'It's been so wonderful. I don't want it to end.'

'Likewise, cherie,' Charles replied, 'but I will see you again soon. Maybe there will be another dance in the future, who knows?'

They bade each other a polite goodnight under the watchful eyes of the guard, then Rachel headed home. As she left, she was aware of the same scowling warder watching her closely. His chilly stare penetrated her warm glow of joy, but she decided to ignore it. What was wrong with him, she wondered, but dismissed him quickly from her thoughts.

Walking home, she felt like she was still dancing, but this time on air, her happiness as bright as the stars in the night sky up above.

Chapter 14

The bright cold days of early March gave way to a damp misty greyness which seeped into the very bones. Wreaths of low cloud hung over the fens, and everything dripped with water. On visiting Rose, a couple of weeks after the dance, Rachel was alarmed to find her friend in bed again, coughing and feverish.

'It's just a cold,' claimed Rose. 'Nothing to worry about.'

But Rachel did worry. There was a pallor to Rose's cheek and a dullness to her eyes. Rachel made her beef tea and brought in some extra firewood to stoke up the stove. Though she went out walking with Charles that afternoon, she felt uneasy in her heart.

Over the last couple of weeks Rachel had remained in a golden bubble of happiness, with her memories of that wonderful night. Charles said he hoped it might happen again but somehow Rachel knew it never would. It was a moment she would always cherish, but she doubted it could ever be repeated.

Rachel's concern for Rose drove her to visit more regularly, but to her dismay the old lady appeared to be going downhill more every day.

Arriving one afternoon for her rendezvous with Charles, Rachel was alarmed to find that Rose did not answer her knock on the door, nor was it unlocked like it normally was.

Becoming frantic she peered through the tiny windows trying to see what was happening. Charles arrived and realising the emergency forced open the front door. The house was silent, and Rachel rushed upstairs to find Rose in bed, sweating with fever and unconscious. Pneumonia had taken her in its grip.

'I'll fetch a doctor,' cried Charles and sped off, returning half an hour later with the same. Meanwhile Rachel mopped Rose's brow with cool rags and tried to get her roused enough to drink some water. Rose stirred and muttered something, but her eyes were glazed and her speech incoherent.

'Hold on, dear Rose,' whispered Rachel, 'help is on its way.'

The doctor, however, sighed and shook his head sadly when he saw the patient.

'Be prepared for the worst, Miss,' he warned Rachel. 'She is elderly and frail, I'm afraid. Her chances are slim.'

Charles stayed there as long as he could, supporting and comforting his beloved, a tower of strength to her in her hour of need. He cursed his situation when he had to leave her alone to nurse her friend.

Not worrying about her commitments at work, Rachel sat with Rose throughout her final hours, doing her best to soothe and calm the old lady and to ease her suffering. At about one o'clock in the morning Rose came to briefly.

'Dear Rachel,' she murmured, 'How kind. What a dear girl. You have always been so good to me.'

'My dearest friend,' replied Rachel, 'you must rest and get well. We need you.'

Rose smiled and slipped into unconsciousness again, with

Rachel holding her hand. Unfortunately, in the early hours she passed away. Dawn came slowly, with a deathly silent chill which Rachel faced alone. Distraught, she notified the undertakers as soon as she could, and once they had arrived to take care of Rose's body, she returned sadly to her duties at the vicarage, not having slept at all. Polly and Kitty were wondering where she was, after she failed to return the evening before.

'You alright, ma'am?' enquired Kitty anxiously as Rachel wearily started the day's chores. 'We was gonna get the constable out looking for you if you hadn't appeared soon.'

Rachel merely nodded at Kitty and mechanically went about her work. Tears wouldn't come at that stage. She felt numb with pain. As the day wore on, however, grief began to overwhelm her, and Rachel retired to her housekeeper's room where she cried a great deal.

Charles had been forced to return to the depot the day before, not knowing (but fearing) the outcome. On his stall in the marketplace, he turned it over in his mind and knew that he had to be with Rachel. A brief visit to Rose's cottage, seeing the black crepe draped over the door handle, established all he needed to know, and he headed immediately to the vicarage. It was quite late in the afternoon, and he knew he was running out of time. Under the terms of his parole, he had to be back at the camp by 7 o'clock and it was already half past five. Not only that, but he was limited to stay within a mile of the great turnpike road, which the vicarage was well beyond. Kitty opened the back door, and recognising him, she gestured for him to follow her to the garden.

'I dunno what you want, but I guess you're here to see the missus,' she said. 'You'd best not be seen, else you'll both be in deep trouble.'

Charles gazed at her, thankful for her kindness.

'Please, yes, Mam'selle Alderman. I think she is upset, and I should see her. Please.'

Kitty frowned.

'Yes, she's real down in the dumps. It wasn't you done upset her, was it?'

'Non, non! Her friend - she has died. I must see her. Please!'

'I'll fetch her. Stay here, out of sight.'

Rachel was red eyed with weeping when Kitty knocked on her door.

'Mrs Alderman,' said Kitty confidentially. 'There's someone 'ere to see you. A good friend – if you know what I mean - of foreign persuasion. He's in the kitchen garden waiting for you.'

The maid turned and left before Rachel had a chance to reply. She was astonished to think that Kitty had been complicit in allowing Charles to visit, but she didn't hesitate to go and find him. His loving arms encircled her grief and gave her much needed comfort. Charles was upset too. They owed Rose a lot and she had been such a lovely person. Fine, decent, caring.

'She was my only friend,' sobbed Rachel, 'and she understood me so well.'

Charles could find no words to say that would ease her pain, so he just held her silently, for a long time. The sun began to sink in the sky and Charles suddenly realised the lateness of the hour.

'Mon Dieu! It is nearly 7 o'clock! Forgive me my darling. I will have to run, or I will be punished for being late back.'

He sprinted all the way back to Norman Cross, but even so it was five past seven by the time he reached the gates. A guard promptly reported this, and it was the black hole again for him. Only 24 hours this time, thankfully, but also a week's loss of parole, meaning he couldn't leave the camp. Sitting in the inky blackness, Charles bemoaned his bad fortune. How could he be there for Rachel when he couldn't even leave the site? It was then that he truly realised the limitations of his present life and felt unworthy to be loved by another such as her. He had nothing to offer her – no prospects, no reliability and no guarantees. Whatever did she see in him?

Staggering out of the black hole the next day, Charles knew he had to get a note to Rachel to explain his absence. His only real hope of this was fellow prisoner Jean Marie Robertson (also known as Black Jemmy), a French officer of uncertain character, who was always asking Charles for favours.

'Jemmy, mon ami,' he began. 'Please can you take a letter for me when you go into town today.'

'Well, yes, of course,' replied Black Jemmy smoothly. 'What's it worth?'

'Well, I, I can give you my turn of exchange,' promised Charles.

Prisoners were on a list, to be exchanged with British POWs when the time came. People often gave others their turn in order to get favours. However, Frenchmen were bottom of the exchange list, as everyone knew, well after the Dutch, the Spanish and the Italians, as the authorities still considered them likely to cause trouble.

'Pooh! What use is that?' said Jemmy. 'We all know we'll never get out! No. I was thinking more about some help with a little business venture I have going.'

'If it's the straw plait trade, forget it!' Charles said forcefully. 'That's illegal and can only lead to trouble. I've heard you're involved.'

Prisoners were strictly forbidden to participate in the manufacture or selling of straw plait (used for making baskets and hats), as it was a thriving industry in the neighbourhood, and the authorities feared local resentment if the POWs started trading. It was one of the more lucrative occupations in Peterborough, especially for women and children, and had saved many a family from the poorhouse. Any inmates found to be involved in this could expect a very harsh punishment.

'Non, non! Nothing like that,' claimed Jemmy. 'Look, I will deliver your letter and then we will work it out later, yes?'

Charles was forced to agree, though to what, he wasn't quite sure. Still, he had little choice, so he handed over the note and prayed that it would arrive in the right hands. He was loathe to tell Black Jemmy much about the recipient, but it seemed the other man had guessed, for he went off laughing to himself.

'Take care with that man,' Johannes warned when he told him. 'He is a very bad lot. I wish I could have helped but as you know I do not get parole like you, as I am not an officer.'

The note was safely delivered, and Rachel realised the next week had to be survived on her own. It was hard but she made the necessary arrangements for her friend's funeral. There seemed to be no family, though there were many friends, mostly from Rose's working life, who helped keep vigil in those first few days. Rose's body was to lie in her cottage until the day of the funeral itself, as was tradition, in a room draped all in black cloth. The elderly housekeeper had been forward thinking enough to pay into a 'burial club' which supplied just enough funds for a simple service and burial; at least it wouldn't be a pauper's grave. Thankfully this meant the grave was less likely to be robbed. Rachel shuddered to think of the body snatchers getting hold of her dear friend's remains. It was such a common occurrence these days.

She planned the event for a few days after Charles' punishment was due to end, for she desperately wanted him to be there. The only thing she hoped was that her own family would not hear about it and decide to attend. Elizabeth and Sarah both knew Rose slightly from the time when Rachel had been so very ill and had kept in touch with her on an occasional basis ever since. It could be very awkward, Rachel thought and hoped they would not find out. Fate, however, is a fickle mistress and a few days later Sarah appeared at the vicarage to offer her sympathies.

'Aunty Rachel! I've just heard about poor dear Rose. How are you? I know you were very close.'

Thinking about it all again made Rachel tearful, and she was glad of Sarah's support. The obvious question arose during their conversation.

'When is the funeral? I'd like to pay my respects.'

Rachel hesitated but had to tell her niece. How could she not?

'Er, well Wednesday, but it'll only be a very small affair. Very simple.'

'I'll be there, Aunty dear, if only to look after you,' Sarah promised, with all good intentions.

Rachel felt dismayed inside. How could this work? She couldn't think.

Sarah left soon afterwards reassuring her aunt that she would be there for her on Wednesday. Rachel hoped she would see Charles again on Monday before the date of the funeral. If she could warn him – maybe – but what could she do? She didn't want to keep him away, but his prison uniform was so noticeable that there was no chance that Sarah wouldn't spot him and react accordingly. Rachel loved them both and felt desperate.

Monday came and Charles returned, much to Rachel's joy. They met at Rose's cottage, but it was strange and forlorn. It felt so wrong to be there with their dear friend's body lying in the front room. The stove was unlit, the bedroom empty and silent. Something had left the dwelling, never to return. Rachel felt waves of grief wash over her.

'Dear Charles,' she said, 'I cannot stay here. Let's walk outside.' Charles agreed, but just as they were leaving a tall man with an imperious manner swooped down upon them.

'Excuse me Madam,' he said. 'You do know this house will need to be emptied and the keys returned by the end of this week, don't you?'

'No, no, I didn't,' said Rachel, 'but of course, I understand.'

'Someone else will be moving in shortly,' the man said. 'I offer you my condolences for your loss, but you need to clean and vacate as soon as possible.'

'Yes, of course,' murmured Rachel. She had known that the house would now pass to someone else, but it was hard all the same. So soon! It didn't seem right. It also held so many happy memories for her and Charles. It had been their refuge, their tiny piece of privacy and happiness. It was going to be a wrench. Not only that but she would have to sort through all Rose's meagre belongings; clothes, mementoes, and such, which would be heart-breaking.

When the man left, she broke down in Charles' arms.

'What can I do? It will be so hard going through everything.'

'I will help you, my cherie,' Charles promised. 'These tasks are better with two, I am thinking. Maybe after the funeral?'

'Ah, no,' said Rachel tearfully. 'Maybe the day after, but, oh that is another problem. I can hardly bear to tell you!'

Charles gazed at her. 'There is something worrying you?'

'Yes! Oh, it is so unfair. I don't know what to do, but my niece Sarah found out and she wants to come to the funeral as well.'

She paused, letting the realisation of what this meant sink in. There was an awkward silence. Then Charles said in a strained voice:

'So, you think I shouldn't be there, then? In case it causes trouble.'

'No! Yes, oh I don't know!' cried Rachel. 'I want you there with me, but if Sarah sees you, well…' Her words trailed off.

They sat on a wooden bench by the river, their heads bowed by misery. For a few minutes neither spoke, each deep in thought.

'I really want to be there,' said Charles quietly, 'to pay my respects to dear Rose, and also to give you my support, but if I must stay away, so be it.'

'No!' exclaimed Rachel. 'There must be something we can do. Have you any other clothes you could wear?'

'Rien! Nothing.' Charles replied, shaking his head.

'I'm wondering,' said Rachel thoughtfully, 'if I could get you an old overcoat or something to cover up your uniform. Then maybe if you stayed back a bit, Sarah wouldn't notice.'

A quick visit to the marketplace offered Rachel a chance to buy an old coat, hat and some second-hand trousers. Between them they hatched a plot to disguise Charles and pass him off as an ex-workmate of Rose's. Rachel returned to the vicarage that evening, feeling happier. All she could hope was that their plan would work, and their relationship would remain undiscovered. A faint hope maybe, but the best she had.

Chapter 15

Wednesday was fast approaching, and Rachel was torn by her duty to the vicarage and her duty to her friend. She couldn't be in two places at once, she knew, so she decided to beg for a few days holiday. There had never been an occasion in the 6 years that she had worked there that she had asked for extra time off. Rachel hoped, therefore, that the parson would be understanding, and she made an appointment to see him. The Reverend was in the parlour with his sister, now a married lady of course, visiting to take tea. He was a kindly (if puritanical) sort of man and he listened politely to Rachel's request.

'My friend Rose; it's her funeral this week and she has no family. I have to be there to arrange everything, and so I was wondering if I could have a few days off, please, Sir?'

In the past Rachel would never have felt confident enough to have asked for something for herself, but she had changed recently. What had happened? she thought.

'Time off!' exclaimed Mrs Holland, 'surely that can't be allowed, Frederick. It's not the 'done thing' for servants!'

The Reverend Tutte raised his hand to hush her.

'Letitia, my dear sister, I do feel Mrs Alderman has performed such wonderful service over the years that she should be permitted this indulgence.'

'Humph!' snorted Letitia. 'Real ladies do not attend funerals. They are of too delicate a sensibility for such ordeals.'

'Sister dear,' the Reverend continued, 'It is up to Mrs Alderman to decide that for herself.'

He turned to Rachel.

'Of course, you may have the time. Take three days off. You will need to rest after such a stressful occasion. We will expect you again on Saturday.'

Rachel thanked him and left the room. Unfortunately, that meant her wages would be considerably less that week, but she was careful with money so she would get by.

The next thing she needed to do was to make sure that the household would run smoothly without her, so that was what she set about arranging that afternoon. Menus were planned, food ordered, bills paid – there was nothing that anyone would have to worry about. Now she could concentrate on her own affairs.

On Wednesday morning Rachel dressed in black and left the vicarage early to take her place by Rose's body for the last part of the vigil. The room was draped all in black and was so still that Rachel felt even her own breath was too loud. It was a relief when Charles arrived later in the morning to keep her company. To her surprise she found herself laughing as they disguised him in the clothes that she had found for him. Standing back to look at the effect, Rachel exclaimed:

'Dear me! You look like a vagabond!'

'Vagabond?' said Charles confused. He'd never heard that word before. 'What is that?'

'Well – a ruffian, a rogue,' Rachel replied. 'Sorry! I'm sure it will be fine,' she reassured him when he looked worried. 'No-one will notice you.'

Charles stayed in the background as people began to arrive for the funeral. Rachel told them he was an old work colleague of Rose's, and they mostly ignored him. Sarah turned up just before the undertakers arrived and insisted on lending her aunt her arm to lean on. Rachel caught Charles' eye and felt very sorry for him. Left out and ignored – how hard was that? And how sad that it couldn't have been his arm that she leaned on for support.

The plain elm coffin was loaded onto a hearse drawn by black horses and proceeded to the church where it was met at the gate by the vicar. The funeral sermon wasn't long, but it was heartfelt. Rose had been a regular churchgoer and the vicar had counted her as one of his flock. Rachel shed tears as he spoke. She would miss her friend so much. Out of the corner of her eye she caught sight of Charles, his eyes also moist with grief, and she longed to comfort him, but it was not to be.

Returning to Rose's tiny home after the service the guests mingled to take a reviving cup of tea, before departing. At this point, things got rather tricky. Sarah approached Charles and introduced herself.

'My name is Sarah, Rachel's niece. Are you an old friend of Rose's?'

'Yes,' Charles muttered, trying not to let his French accent show. 'An old friend.' He started pretending to cough in order not to speak. Rachel rapidly intervened then, saying 'My dear Mr Smith, please get yourself a drink. Sarah, come and meet Betty who I used to work with; you remember; from the time when I was ill.'

She led her away, hoping Sarah would not pursue her curiosity, and to her relief, her niece was sufficiently distracted to forget about him. Charles melted into the background again, and a short while later, left quietly without anyone noticing.

At the end of the afternoon Rachel was quite exhausted. What with the stress of trying to hide Charles and her grief at Rose's death, she felt almost overwhelmed, and she was relieved she had a day or two to recover. She'd arranged to meet Charles at the cottage on Friday in order to empty it; a job she was not looking forward to. In the meantime, she went to stay with her sister Elizabeth, to relax and to catch up with the family. With Elizabeth's kind attention and homely manner, Rachel soon felt strong enough to tackle this unpleasant task the following day.

'Why don't you let me come with you?' suggested Elizabeth, just as Rachel was planning to leave on Friday morning. 'I did all this for our mother and I'm sure I could help you.'

It's true – Elizabeth had been the one to take care of everything back then, as Rachel was working. The most she had been able to do was to take a half day off to attend the funeral.

'No, no, thank you, but I need to do this alone.' Rachel lied. 'I knew her better than anyone and it should be me, but I appreciate the offer.'

She breathed a sigh of relief when Elizabeth reluctantly let her go. It would have been a disaster if she had seen Charles.

Charles arrived promptly and they began downstairs, cleaning and removing all the household effects. Sadly, Rachel bagged up the cooking pots, plates and utensils to take to a destitute family who lived just down the road. These items did not evoke too much emotion but when they got upstairs to sort through Rose's clothes, Rachel found it all too much. The final straw was coming across Rose's favourite woollen shawl, much patched with the old lady's careful needlework, a loose hair or two still clinging to it, a last memory of a dear friend. Rachel sat down glumly on Rose's humble bed, tears rolling down her face.

'My dearest cherie,' soothed Charles. 'Cry on my shoulder, my pauvre enfant.'

She rested her head against him and let her grief flow, until she felt better. Charles murmured words of love and comfort to her and stroked her hair gently. Suddenly, Rachel was overwhelmed with her love and gratitude for his devotion, and she kissed him desperately, searching for salvation. Charles responded eagerly but after a moment he pulled away, reluctantly, saying: 'Mon cherie, I think we should perhaps carry on with our task.' Rachel gazed at him with surprise.

'I do not want to be taking the advantage of you. You are upset and do not know what you do, maybe.'

He stood up, but Rachel pulled him down again to sit on the bed.

'My darling Charles,' she said, 'I love you so much and I need you. Believe me - I know what I am doing. Hold me close.'

With that they lay down on the bed together, a mutual need for comfort and love swamping them like a giant wave. Rachel had never felt so alive, her body tingling with anticipation and pleasure. Charles gently let his hands wander onto her bosom and things took their natural course. In spite of Rachel's inexperience, the moment, when it came, was an avalanche of sweet passion which swept them both away. Lying there in the aftermath, Rachel shed more tears but this time of joy and relief. Charles held her tightly, hardly believing this could happen. What right had he to this love? he thought. What devil had sent it to him at this time and place to torment and tease him? He knew their love was doomed, and yet he could not deny it. They were meant for each other.

Eventually they sat up, dressed and bravely continued their sad duty. Little was said of what had taken place. Each was filled with too much emotion to be able to express it.

Finally, the house clean and empty, Rachel returned the keys to the empty hearted official who was only too glad to snatch them back.

'The end of an era,' said Charles, looking back as they shut the door for the last time.

'Yes, indeed,' replied Rachel, 'no more meetings there. We will have to go back to outdoors, now. At least the weather is improving.' She felt different. She noted the sweet pain in her body and was glad. A woman at last, she thought, and it pleased her greatly.

'Today may never be able to be repeated,' Charles remarked sadly.

'I know, but at least we have this memory. It's enough.'

He studied her face carefully. 'I hope you are well, and it was not too painful.'

Rachel smiled. 'My dear, it was perfect, more than I could ever have hoped for.' She touched his face lovingly. 'You have changed my life.'

Charles kissed her hand.

'I wish things could be different, but I think that one day I will be sent back to France and that all this will be over.'

'Then we must live for the moment,' said Rachel. 'Today is all that counts.'

They kissed and parted, each to return to their respective prisons, already aware that time was slipping away from them.

Chapter 16

'Boucher! Boucher – come 'ere! What you up to?'

Charles started up at the sound of his name being shouted by the ill-tempered Halliday. Hurrying to the warder, he tried to act as submissively as he knew how.

'Sir, pardon. What can I do?'

Halliday scowled at him.

'You – I know you're up to something. You're never here and yet I don't find you at the market very often. Methinks you're involved in something bad. A wrong 'un, you are!'

'Non, non, Sir. I am there, selling my little toys. You just do not see me.'

'I'll check,' said Halliday unpleasantly, 'and if I find you aren't there, I'll be after you! Remember you only got a mile limit!'

Charles turned away from the warder's wrath, but secretly he was worried. It's true he had been spending a great deal of time with Rachel lately and had hardly been at his market stall at all. He would have to put in an appearance, and make sure Halliday saw him.

'What's he so worked up about?' he asked his friend Johannes.

'Oh, don't you know?' the cheerful Dutchman replied. 'He got caught letting Agné - you know; that wealthy chap from Rennes - meet up with his woman from the town. Charlotte Barker, I think she was called; anyway, Halliday was allowing them to use his turnkey's lodge for their 'meetings', if you know what I mean!'

'Really?' said Charles, amazed.

'Yes, hauled up before Governor Pressland he was, nearly lost his job, I hear.'

'Shame he didn't!' exclaimed Charles. 'He's the bane of my life! But why would he do such a thing? He's not exactly renowned for his kindness and generosity!'

Johannes smiled and rubbed his fingers together. 'Money, my dear friend! What else? Agné has a rich family you know. Making a killing, Halliday was!'

'He's in a worse mood than ever, now, unfortunately,' remarked Charles.

'From what I hear he's been told to crack down hard on us all, or it's out the door for him. No house, no job, no wages!'

Charles groaned. That's all he needed – Halliday on the war path.

Meanwhile, he was also getting pressure from fellow prisoner, Black Jemmy, to take out straw plait goods for him.

'Just take these parcels,' the man coaxed. 'It's nothing to worry about. After all, I did you a favour a while ago, didn't I?'

'I'll think about it,' murmured Charles and sped off. Things were getting hot for him, he thought, and he didn't like it.

It was a fine spring day when Rachel next saw Charles at the market and she was hoping that they could go for a walk somewhere more discreet, but it wasn't to be. She was disappointed but understood. All they could do was to talk at his stall, an arrangement that was far from satisfactory. Rachel got tired of standing up, and so Charles leant her his wooden box to sit on. Normally they tried not to be seen in public together, so they were both nervous and fidgety. Conversation was awkward. The market was busy and crowded and Rachel suddenly realised with horror that Sarah was bearing down upon them. She leapt up and was about to flee but it was too late. Sarah had seen her.

'Aunty! What are you doing here? And who is this?' She turned to Charles. 'I've seen you before, haven't I? Wait a minute – Rose's funeral! Aunty, what are you up to? Why are you with this dirty foreigner? What's going on?'

Her voice was raised angrily. Rachel tried to take her arm and lead her away, but she wasn't having any of it.

'No, no. I want to know! You`re friends with him, aren't you? Don't you know who killed Eddie? How could you?'

Then she demanded accusingly: 'Are you lovers?'

Rachel's face went red with shame and embarrassment.

'Please, Sarah, listen. We're friends, yes. Charles is a good man. It's not his fault Eddie died.'

'Died! He was murdered! By him and his countrymen. What are you doing with him? A good man - huh!'

'Madame, please,' interjected Charles. 'Calm yourself. This lady was just resting here as she was overcome by the sun.'

Sarah turned on him. 'You filthy Frenchman - a likely story! You disgust me. How dare you even speak to me?'

She glared at her aunt.

'I can't understand you,' she said. 'How could you?'

With that she gathered up her skirts and swept off through the busy marketplace.

Rachel looked at Charles.

'I'm sorry,' she said. 'I'll try and explain it to her. Maybe I should follow?'

'Mais, non, it is not a good idea,' said Charles. 'Leave her a while. Perhaps when she has time to think, she may listen.'

'You're probably right,' said Rachel tearfully, 'but I hate to fall out with her. We have been so close in the past. I practically brought her up after her mother died. Oh, how I wish Rose was here. She'd know just what to do.'

After a night of reflection Sarah was feeling calmer the next day. Perhaps she had wronged her aunt. Perhaps she should find out more. Early that morning Sarah made her way to where the Frenchman usually had his stall, but to her surprise he wasn't there. When she enquired at the vegetable stall opposite, she got some unwelcome information.

'Him! Well, I dunno. He's always late and often don't stop 'ere long. He's off with his woman again, I guess.'

(In fact, Charles had been kept back at the camp by Halliday, demanding he sweep the exercise yard a second time).

'Shameful really, that's what it is!' the trader continued.

'His woman?' asked Sarah. 'Who's that?'

'Oh, it's that housekeeper from the vicarage, you know. Mrs Alderman's her name. Claims she's just 'ere to order my veg but I know what she's up to, really. Always round 'im, talking and flirting. Pity that a decent English woman should become a Frenchman's whore!'

144

Incensed, Sarah agreed. So that was the truth of it. Her aunt – a fallen woman! A whore for the enemy! She would never forgive her - never!

It was three days more before Rachel had time to make a much-dreaded visit to Sarah's house. She knocked timidly, her nerves all of a twitter. She had spent much time since their last encounter, turning it over in her mind and rehearsing what she would say. Her intention was to try and be honest about their relationship in the hope that Sarah might realise how lonely Rachel had been until now, and how happy Charles had made her. Perhaps a frank and direct approach would be best, she thought, though her heart trembled at the idea.

Sarah opened the front door, her face set hard as stone. She made no move to invite Rachel in, but simply said: 'Well?'

Rachel's nerve shattered like glass, and her stammer returned.

'Sarah, I, please, I, can we, please, that is, can we talk?'

Rachel's face was beetroot red, and she was sweating. She swallowed hard, trying to pull herself together.

'If we must,' replied Sarah coldly. 'Come in then.'

Sarah lived in a respectable middle-class house which had the luxury of a small front parlour. It was there that they went now and sat down awkwardly. Rachel took a deep breath.

'Sarah, I have to explain,' she began. 'I didn't intend any of this to happen, but I've been on my own for so long. I never thought any man would look at me, after all I know my face is plain and not comely like many maidens. I'm an old, tired spinster who has spent her life looking after other people. Charles was kind enough to be a friend to me. We just talked and well, I suppose, we fell in love.'

After this long and unexpected speech, Rachel's voice trailed off. Sarah stared at her, saying nothing. Rachel felt she had to fill the difficult silence and so continued:

'Charles is a good man. Yes, he is French, I know, but he's just a soldier like anyone else. He has given me so much happiness. I know Eddie was killed, but that's war. Many die on both sides. Eddie would have understood that.'

Sarah glared at her.

'So, you think it fine to be a Frenchman's whore then?'

Rachel gasped. 'It's not like that, Sarah, really.'

'No? Well, that's not what I've heard! You should hear the gossip in the marketplace. Do you deny you are a fallen woman?'

Rachel blushed deeply.

'I cannot pretend that I am 'untouched' anymore, it is true,' she admitted, 'but life is for living.' She paused then said simply: 'I love him, Sarah.'

'You disgust me,' her niece said. 'How can you consort with the enemy? It's not right. Besides, don't you know that one day he will up and leave you without a backward glance?'

'All the more reason to live for today!' retorted Rachel, getting angry.

'Oh, so who told you that that kind of behaviour is acceptable? Him? Or that lowlife friend of yours – Rose?'

'You leave Rose alone!' cried Rachel. 'She was a wonderful friend to me. I miss her so much.'

'Seems to me you keep the wrong company,' said Sarah coldly.

146

'Well, if you want the company of your family you need to get rid of that man! Aunt Elizabeth feels the same as well. I spoke to her about it yesterday and she was shocked by your slatternliness.'

'Is this an ultimatum?' asked Rachel, stunned.

'You could call it that, yes. It's us – your family – or that man. You cannot be part of our lives whilst you are still seeing him. I will not allow my children to be tainted by your sinfulness.'

Rachel had suffered many insults in her life, but she had never felt so angry or hurt before. Her own family were turning their back on her, after all she had done for them. She pleaded with her niece:

'Surely, if you really love me, you can understand and forgive me. Your dear mother would have done, I'm sure.'

Her words fell on deaf ears.

'Forgive? Never! And how dare you mention my mother. You're not worthy to talk of her. Get out and don't come back until you have seen sense!'

Rachel stood up and made for the door, her heart pounding.

'I can never give him up,' she declared as she left. With great dignity she added: 'I'm sorry you all feel this way, but my decision is made.'

A sudden rain shower fell as she headed back to the vicarage, mirroring the tears streaming down her face. Her heavy silk dress was wet and coated with mud by the time she arrived, but she took little notice of it. Her thoughts were too preoccupied with her family. She'd lost them, she knew. Even if they reconciled, things would never be the same. But Charles was the love of her life and meant more to her than anyone, or

147

anything. She'd never wanted it to come to this, she thought. Why couldn't they just accept the situation and wish her well? Was it so unreasonable?

Remembering her dear departed sister Mary, Rachel wondered whether she would indeed have approved of the choices that she had made. Somehow, she felt that Mary would have understood. She had always told Rachel that love was the most important thing of all. If only the rest of her family would see it that way.

That night, sleep eluded her, and she was tormented by memories and regret. Why was the world so unfair?

Chapter 17

Black Jemmy was hovering in the doorway as Charles entered the barracks a few days later. There were several other inmates around, so Charles wasn't unduly worried, however one sharp word from Jemmy meant that they beat a hasty retreat, and he was left alone with him.

'Le Boucher,' Jemmy said smoothly, 'just the man I needed to see. I have a little job for you, a favour in return, if you like.'

Charles tried to appear non-committal.

'Oh, yes? How can I help.'

'I think you know what I'd like you to do,' the man continued. 'I have a parcel I need taken out. Just take it to your stall in the market and someone will collect it from you. Simple.'

'What's in it?' asked Charles, though in his heart he already knew.

'You don't need to know,' growled Jemmy.

'Well, but I do, because I don't want to get involved in anything dubious. You know Halliday's out for my blood.' He lowered his voice. 'If it's straw plait, it's too risky.'

'Nothing like that,' said Jemmy persuasively. 'Just some food stuffs for a friend. No need to worry.'

'Let me see it then,' Charles replied. He wasn't going to get caught that easily.

'Non, non, it is all wrapped up now. It would spoil.'

'Well, I'm sorry. I'd like to help but I'm not doing it without seeing it.'

Suddenly Jemmy flew into a rage. He grabbed Charles by the shirt collar and pulled him towards him roughly.

'Are you trying to be funny? You owe me, remember!'

'Yes, yes, of course, and if there's anything else I can do, but not this, please Jemmy!'

Just then Johannes came in the blockhouse. The Dutchman was tall and muscular and loomed large in the doorway.

'What's going on?' he asked.

Jemmy released Charles abruptly.

'Nothing, nothing,' he said, 'just a bit of friendly banter.' He turned to go but as he left, he added to Charles in a low voice: 'I'll be back. You better watch yourself!'

Charles heaved a sigh of relief when he had gone.

'Thanks Johannes. Things were getting nasty.'

'He is a bad man.' Johannes sighed. 'Be careful. There's a rumour he murdered the previous captain on his ship, in order to get promotion.'

It was only a couple of days later when Charles was in the marketplace again that things developed further. A rough looking character appeared to be browsing his stall for a long period of time and Charles became suspicious and a bit concerned. Today was a day when he was not seeing Rachel as she was busy working, but at least the weather was dry, and he was doing his best to sell his wares. It had been quite a successful morning so far. The man (hard faced and caked with grime) seemed to have no interest in buying, and yet he was hanging around. Why? thought Charles and wondered if his takings were safe. The reason became apparent as soon as there was no-one else in sight.

'Hey you. I got something for you,' said the man gruffly. 'Take this.'

He thrust a large package at him.

'What's this?' Charles asked, confused.

'Ask no questions, you get no lies,' replied the man. 'Just pass it to Jemmy, when you get back, that's all.'

Charles' heart sank. Oh no!

'I can't do that,' he said.

The man came very close to him, and Charles could smell his sweat and hear his heavy breathing. All of a sudden, he was aware of a knife held next to his ribs. He froze.

'You will do this,' the man said forcefully, 'or it will be the worse for you. Get it?'

Charles just nodded silently, afraid to move or speak. The man released him and moved off down the aisle leaving the parcel conspicuously on Charles' stall. He grabbed it quickly and moved it out of sight. He realised his hands were perspiring and his heart was pounding. How close he had come to death, he hated to think. But now what? What could he do? Charles was no coward, but he didn't want to get in this much trouble. It could mean being sent to the hulks if he was caught having anything to do with the straw plait trade. He packed up his stall early that day – he needed time to think. The parcel was tucked in his bag, but he hesitated to take it into the camp. Slowly heading back towards Norman Cross, Charles suddenly had an idea. What if he were to 'lose it' on the way back? Maybe he could hide or dump it somewhere and claim it had never been delivered to him. Briefly he debated just throwing it in the river Nene, but there were too many people around and it would make too big a splash. Eventually he managed to hide it in a hedge full of briars thick enough not to reveal the forbidden item. He felt better once it was away from his person, but next there was Black Jemmy to face. He decided just to plead total ignorance and hope for the best.

It wasn't so very long to wait before his fellow prisoner put in an appearance at his blockhouse.

'I don't know what you mean,' said Charles. 'No-one came near. What parcel? Of course, if I'd had it, I'd have brought it to you.'

It fooled Jemmy that day, but not for long, sadly. Two days later Charles was busy cleaning the barracks when he arrived. The rest of the inmates scattered, as if they knew what was coming.

'Thought you'd fool me, didn't you?' the man started angrily. 'Trying to keep stuff for yourself, ain't you? Trying to rip me off! Well, I ain't having it!'

Jemmy let fly with his fist and sent Charles crashing into the wall. Dazed, he fought back, but Jemmy though small, was wiry and strong.

Many blows found their mark on Charles, and he began to stagger. Ironically, it was only the arrival of his nemesis Halliday, that stopped the fight.

'Ere you two. Pack it in. Right, it's the black hole for you, Le Boucher, and half rations for you Robertson! That'll sort you both out.'

Protesting at the unfairness Charles was dumped into the lonely darkness with little more than bread and water. Despite this, it was a welcome relief to be away from Jemmy. At least he couldn't get him in there. Two days later, Charles was out and able to return to his market stall. Rachel was shocked to see his bruises and concerned for him. Reluctantly, he related what had happened.

'Surely you should tell someone?' she suggested.

Charles laughed bitterly.

'Who? Halliday hates my guts anyway and if I went to someone else, I'd be seen as a snitch. Life wouldn't be worth living around the camp. We all know what goes on, but we don't tell. It's asking for trouble.'

Rachel sympathised and soothed him as best she could.

'Please be careful, my love,' she said. 'I hate to think of you being hurt.'

'I'll be fine, cherie. Do not worry,' he reassured her, but he didn't feel too sure of that.

His bruises fading slowly, Charles did his best to keep out of Black Jemmy's way. This was easier said than done, however. Though the depot was large and sprawling, it was easy enough to find someone if you looked hard enough. A few days went by, and Charles was beginning to relax. Surely things were good again now. He was busy mopping the floor of the blockhouse when Johannes suddenly came tearing in, his normally placid face beset with worry and alarm.

'Quick, my friend! I fear the worst. Jacques Bouvier told me that Jemmy has had something planted in here to land you in the hot water. Not only that but there's a bunk inspection in an hour!'

Charles and Johannes turned the place upside down in their efforts to find the item. Time was running short when they finally found it attached to the underside of Charles' bunk.

'Now what?' said Charles desperately, sweating in panic. 'Where can we get rid of it? What can we do?'

Johannes grabbed it and ran off, leaving Charles to do his best to straighten up the place. He never found out where his friend disposed of it, but the camp incinerator burned a bit brighter that day, and the inspection was happily without incident.

Jemmy's rage was unabated, however, and only a day later Charles was hauled up before Governor Pressland himself. Halliday had great glee in marching him over to the office.

'You're for it, this time, Le Boucher. Serves you right!'

Charles' mind raced. What had the unpleasant inmate said or done? How could he defend himself? Certainly, the charge was an unexpected one.

Pressland gazed sternly at Charles. He had been the agent at Norman Cross for several years now and had seen many men come through his office. Despite his demeanour he was a hard-working family man who did his best by the inmates whenever he could. However, he had to uphold the rules.

'Le Boucher, I am informed that you have abused the privileges of your parole conditions and have travelled outside the one-mile limit.'

'Non, Monsieur Governor, I beg your pardon,' began Charles. 'Mais non, certainement, non!'

Though he knew this was true on several occasions, he certainly wasn't going to own up to it. Surely there was no proof.

'Who said this?' he asked.

'You do not need to know,' said the governor. 'It is enough that it has been said.'

'But Monsieur, this is not true! Where is the proof?'

'Do not try to be impertinent with me, Sir! What I say goes in this camp. Your parole has been cancelled permanently. Think yourself lucky you have not received a stiffer penalty. Dismissed!'

'Cancelled! No, Monsieur, please, no,' Charles pleaded. 'At least let me earn my parole again in the future. Give me a chance please.'

Pressland hesitated. He was a fair man though strict. He re-read the report which he had been given but could see only tales of bad character from Charles' warder, Halliday, which added to his decision.

'From what I see here you have a bad reputation as a troublemaker and rogue, fighting in camp, being rude to your betters and worse. Listen to what I say, Le Boucher and believe me: your parole has been cancelled forthwith on a permanent basis. There will be no more leaving the depot for you. Now get out.'

Charles returned to his barracks, feeling stunned. Never to leave camp again, never to see Rachel, to touch her, to hold her in his arms. How could he survive? To only see the outside world through the gaps in the perimeter wall – how could he manage? What's more he couldn't even let Rachel know. He sank his head in his hands in despair.

Chapter 18

Three weeks went by, and Rachel began to feel seriously worried. She was used to Charles being absent from his market stall from time to time, usually because Halliday's vindictiveness had landed her beloved in the black hole again. But it had never been this long before. Knowing Charles to be in conflict with Black Jemmy as well, her stomach knotted up with dread when she yet again found only an empty space where Charles' stall should be. It's no good, she thought. I have to find out what's going on. I will go to the depot and ask for information. I just hate to think of him ill, or injured, or, or….worse. I need to know.

Meanwhile, Charles had been going through his own private hell. He longed for the fresh air and open spaces, but most of all he longed to see Rachel. It gnawed away at him, turning him into an angry and desperate man. The slightest provocation sent him flying into a rage which was most unlike him. What would his lover do, he wondered, when he didn't turn up? Would she think he had abandoned her? He hoped with all his heart that she wouldn't. Each day he went forlornly to the outer camp perimeter. Higher than a man's head and solidly built, the wall was nevertheless crumbling in many places, due to the relentless pounding on it by the prisoners. Those inmates who did not have the luxury of parole, attempted to see the outside world by peering through the gaps, but all they could see were mere glimpses of the customers on the other side. Stalls were set up on the outside by two prisoners each time, which allowed the exchange of goods and monies, but they were not allowed to mix with the public. Once set up they were closely guarded to ensure no mingling took place. Even so, Charles hoped and prayed that maybe his turn would come. Today, however, all he could do was to gaze out of one of the many holes in the brick wall, hoping against hope for some sight of his beloved, unlikely though that seemed.

Rachel made her way slowly to Norman Cross, her heart feeling heavier with every step. A fine mist was lying low over the fens as she walked, her hair soon dampened by the moisture and her spirits equally low. Was Charles alright? Why had he not come? So many thoughts ran through her head.

She approached the east gate and saw a minor hubbub along the road. Ah yes, the prison market, that was it. Maybe if she could speak to someone, they would know something. It was noisy and crowded with members of the public jostling around the stalls and the guards patrolling up and down, eyeing people suspiciously. Rachel attempted to push her way through, but it was a struggle. She was left outside on the edge wandering along the outskirts looking for someone to talk to. Eventually she spied a guard briefly alone and she approached him.

'Sir. I am looking for news of a friend, Monsieur Charles Le Boucher. Do you know of him?'

The guard snorted derisively.

'Huh! Is he a prisoner here?'

'Yes,' she replied, 'but he has parole.'

'You think I know them all by name, lady? There are 5000 men here. Think again!'

He marched off and Rachel was no further forward in her search for Charles. There were voices shouting from the walls and she glanced up but could not see her dearest one. Too many people and too much noise – how would she ever find him in this? She wandered dejectedly back along the road and finally managed to squeeze into a space by one of the stalls. A grimy looking inmate clad in the usual yellow, was behind the wares.

'Excuse me,' she said. 'Have you seen my friend Charles Le Boucher?'

The man scowled. His English wasn't good, and he only wanted to sell his goods, not chat with people. He shook his head and turned away. However, a voice from behind her suddenly asked:

'What do you want with that scoundrel?'

It was Halliday, Charles' persecutor. Rachel, however, was so pleased to have found someone who knew him that she turned gratefully and said:

'Do you know him? Is he well? Why has he not been to the market?'

Halliday regarded her with contempt. 'Him? He's not going outside any more now. Parole's been cancelled for that rogue and serves him right! I guess you know the reason why. You look a decent woman but you're just like all the rest, ain't you? A Frenchman's whore!'

With that he walked off leaving Rachel in pieces. Parole cancelled! How would she ever see him?

She consoled herself with the thought that at least he was well. Halliday's insult barely touched her, she was more concerned about Charles. Deciding she would get nothing else that day, she walked sadly back to the city.

Charles meanwhile, thought he had spotted her passing by, but though he called and shouted desperately, she was too far away to hear him above the noise of the crowd. Maybe he had been mistaken, he thought, after all, why would she come here? Nevertheless, to think of her so tantalisingly close and yet so far away, tormented him long into the night.

The next day Johannes found Charles sitting on his bunk, staring into space.

'Heh, my friend! Get up. Don't you know Halliday is on the warpath again? If he sees you here, you're for it!'

Reluctantly Charles rose and started his daily chores, but his mind wasn't on it. Johannes teased him gently.

'Come on, my friend, you've done that three times now.' Then more kindly, he asked: 'What is the matter? I am thinking you are not yourself.'

Johannes knew Charles had been seeing Rachel but not how serious it had become. He was shocked to see a tear escape from his comrades' eye as he spoke.

'Oh Johannes, I cannot help it. I miss her so much.'

'Your English lady?'

'Yes, my dearest Rachel. I'm sure I saw her yesterday by the market. I called and called her, but she never heard me, stuck behind that dratted wall.'

'Would she really come here?'

'Maybe. She must be wondering what has happened to me. She will be worried.'

'My friend,' said Johannes, his voice anxious, 'would it not better to let her go? You know there is no future for the two of you, together. I'm sorry but that's the hard truth.'

'Never!' declared Charles. 'I can never let her go. We belong together. You don't understand!'

'My dear friend, forgive me! I believe you. If it is true love, which I think it must be, then there is no giving it up. That is why my dear wife, Maria, came here with me. We could not bear to be apart.'

'So, help me,' begged Charles. 'There must be something we can do. If I could only get a letter through to her, somehow.'

Johannes thought for a moment.

'Well,' he said, 'I cannot leave the camp, but Maria – maybe I could ask her. She goes into town once a week. Though she speaks no English, so it may be difficult.'

'Really?' said Charles, his face brightening. 'I could write her a note and give her the address. That would be wonderful. At least my love would know what has happened. Thank you!'

Sunk in gloom, Rachel presented a cold and stony-faced demeanour to her work colleagues, who remarked on it privately later.

'Er's in one of 'er funny moods again,' said Polly, busy chopping up the meat for dinner.

'Well, you know what she's like,' replied Kitty. 'Bit of a deep one, but pretty decent to us, all the same.' (She had a bit of a soft spot for her boss).

'Humph. Well, she better be, that's all I say. Don't know what's eating 'er'.

Kitty smiled to herself as she peeled the potatoes. She had her own ideas on the matter; an affair of the heart, she guessed, with that Frenchman, probably. Still, that was their business and best kept quiet, so she said nothing.

It was two lonely days before Rachel heard anything. Turning things over and over in her mind she was resolved to go back to the camp on her next afternoon off and try again. There must be some way of finding Charles. She was delighted therefore when Kitty came running up to her housekeeper's office to tell her she had a visitor.

'Some foreign lady, Mrs Alderman. Don't seem to speak no English, just keeps saying your name.'

Poor Maria had been strictly instructed to deliver the letter in person to Rachel and no-one else, so she clung to it bravely in spite of Kitty's entreaties. Rachel went to the door and saw a small, dark haired young woman, neatly but plainly dressed and clearly very nervous. Rachel tried her best to put her at ease.

'Madam,' she began, 'How can I help you?'

Maria looked confused, not understanding what was said, clutching a piece of paper tightly in her hands.

'Mevrouw Alderman? Rachel Alderman?'

'Yes, that's me. Is that for me?' Rachel said, pointing and nodding vigorously to show that she was indeed the person that Maria wanted. She held out her hand and Maria handed over the letter with relief, then turned and fled.

'Thank you,' Rachel called after her then hurried inside to read it. It was short and to the point. Charles' written English was not as good as his spoken language, but Rachel read that his parole was cancelled and that he would be at a certain gap in the wall each afternoon at 3 o'clock, unless prevented by circumstance. She now knew where to look for him as he had given her directions. What a relief! She would see him at last.

It was a bright spring day as Rachel hurried to the camp two days later. She was desperate to see Charles again and full of hope that they could spend time chatting. She made her way eagerly to the gap Charles had directed her to but was disappointed. It was such a small hole in the crumbling perimeter, merely a couple of dislodged bricks. She could see very little although she could hear French voices the other side. There seemed to be some sort of argument going on, however she suddenly recognised her loved one's voice and called out impulsively:

'Charles – I am here!'

There were sounds of scuffling and pushing the other side, then finally Charles appeared at the hole in the wall. She could only just see his face, but it was a welcome sight, none the less.

'My darling. Cherie,' he called. 'I have had to fight my way through to get here. I fear we do not have long to talk. I miss you.'

He attempted to put his hand through the small gap but only managed a few fingers. Rachel grasped them and kissed them fervently.

'My dearest Charles, this is awful. How can we manage like this? Must it go on? Is there anything you can do?'

'I fear not, my love,' he replied. 'There is just one small hope and that is that each week different prisoners get selected to come out and run the stall outside. If only I can get onto the list, then we could meet properly. I am so sorry.'

'Why has this happened?' asked Rachel. Charles told her the details and she immediately felt bad about it.

'It is all my fault,' she declared. 'If you hadn't come over to the vicarage, it would have been alright. How dreadful!'

'It cannot be helped,' said Charles. 'What gets me is the fact that someone told on me, and the governor believed them even though there's no proof. I begged him to allow me to earn my parole again but it's no good. Halliday has told him I'm a bad lot, so he won't listen.'

'Maybe if I went to see him…' began Rachel, but Charles laughed bitterly.

'A nice idea, my darling, but the prison doesn't exactly encourage 'relationships' between inmates and civilians. Everyone knows it goes on, but the authorities can't be seen to approve of it.'

He kissed Rachel's fingertips through the hole in the bricks.

'I wish I could hold you again,' he said wistfully. 'I feel lost without you.'

'I am here, my love,' she replied. 'No matter what.'

Just then there was more kerfuffle on the other side of the wall and Charles disappeared from view. He had been shoved violently aside by another inmate also desperate to see the outside world. Rachel was shocked to see a strange face suddenly appear.

'Bonjour, Mam'selle!' the stranger said leering at her, but was then forcibly pushed away himself, by Charles regaining his position.

'I have to go, cherie,' Charles told her sadly. 'There are too many others who want the same thing. But please come again if you can. It's better than nothing.'

Rachel promised him that she would, then bade him a reluctant farewell and left. Charles waved to her through the tiny hole in the wall, feeling a terrible sense of loss and loneliness as he watched her walk away.

Chapter 19

Three miserable weeks went by. Rachel and Charles attempted to meet but the encounters were not satisfying. Sometimes there were so many other prisoners on the inside that Charles was pushed away. At other times they enjoyed a few brief moments of privacy before having to part, feeling worse than ever. Each meeting seemed to make it harder than ever, and they both felt angry and frustrated. It was then that something happened that made Charles think deeply about his situation. Johannes came into his bunk house one morning:

'Heh,' he said, 'did you hear? Ducross escaped last night. Impersonated a guard, so they say!'

'Really?' replied Charles. 'Have they caught him yet?'

Escape attempts were frequent, but usually unsuccessful.

'No. They reckon he's on his way to the coast to get a boat to France.'

'He'll never make it,' Charles said. 'They always catch them in the end. Still – it's almost worth it, just to be free for a few days.'

A week went by and the whole prison was abuzz with talk of the escape. He still hadn't been picked up yet.

'Someone's helping on the outside, they reckon,' said Johannes, 'maybe a woman. That's what you need, someone with contacts and money.'

This set Charles to thinking. How he longed to be free of here.

Wouldn't it be wonderful to take off somewhere with Rachel, to start a new life? Once he got this idea in his head it was hard to dismiss. It inhabited his mind. If only, he thought, if only. Still, he reasoned, Rachel probably wouldn't want to go off with him as his mistress, and who could blame her? But he knew that they could be happy together, away from his wife and away from here.

On a gloriously sunny morning in early May Charles finally got his turn to man the stall outside. True, he had bribed one of the guards in order to jump the queue, but he didn't care. It felt so good to be out in the fresh air again, not hemmed in by walls and barricades. Rachel turned up later that day and was delighted to see him properly for once. Nevertheless, she was worried by his haggard face, and he in turn, noticed some grey hairs on her head that hadn't been there before. This stress was getting to them both. Conversation was still difficult however, with the constant supervision of the guards, plus the jostle of customers eager to get a bargain. Even so, they managed some words in quieter moments.

'Cherie,' Charles said when the guard was off checking elsewhere, 'how would you like to come away with me and start a new life?'

Rachel laughed. He was joking surely, or daydreaming. 'Well of course, my love, but that's not going to happen, is it?'

Charles hesitated. 'But what if it could? Would you do it? Would you come away with me?'

Rachel was confused. Why was he asking her something that could never happen?

'Well, yes, I would,' she replied, 'but it's just a dream, Charles. Let's be realistic.'

He whispered to her now. 'I'm serious, Rachel. What if I were to…escape?'

Escape! Rachel was so shocked that she nearly said it out loud, but she stopped herself just in time. Keeping her voice low, she said:

'But Charles, how? Surely it is not possible.'

'Many have done it in the past, my love, and one very recently. Sometimes they are caught and brought back, but sometimes not.'

'I don't know, Charles. It is dangerous. You might get killed or something.'

'Don't worry about me,' Charles said grimly. 'All I need to know is whether you would come with me. There's no point otherwise.'

'But where would we go?' she asked.

'Into the countryside. Maybe we could find work on a farm. We could live our lives together. I know it's a lot to ask. Please say you'll think about it.'

Rachel merely nodded, as just then the guard returned, rendering further discussion impossible. Her mind reeled and she needed space to think. Her feelings for Charles were not in doubt, but still, to give up her present life and flee with him as fugitives – what an idea!

Walking slowly back to the vicarage her thoughts were in a whirl. Her dream had always been to live with Charles, as his common law wife. She knew it was impossible for them to marry and that in the eyes of the world it was wrong, but this didn't worry her. Her love for Charles surpassed all this. Did this mean she was immoral, she wondered. A sinner? Probably, she thought; still, so be it. The things that did concern her though were issues like her loyalty to her employer and fellow workers. Foolish perhaps, but Rachel had been there a long time and felt a strong attachment to them all. Then there was her family; but they had already rejected her as a fallen woman anyway. Even so, she had hoped to rebuild her relationships with them one day. She still loved them in spite of their disapproval of her. There would be no way back to them if she went ahead with this.

Mechanically Rachel set about her evening chores when she got back. It was all routine to her anyway. Then she sat in her housekeeper's room at the end of the day, trying to work out what to do.

Peterborough - it was the only place she'd ever lived apart from her brief stay in London. She knew nothing of the rest of the countryside. What's more, the only jobs she had ever done had been domestic. How could she work on a farm? And without a reference, what work could she get? Rachel tried to sleep but everything was going around her head and she arose at the usual hour of 5.30am having barely slept a wink. Kitty, ever observant, noticed something was wrong.

'You alright, Ma'am? You look a bit peaky if you don't mind me saying.'

Rachel did her best to reassure the maid but felt so tired she could hardly stand. Her hands trembled and she could barely lift the tray to take the morning tea up to the Reverend.

'Let me do that,' suggested Kitty, kindly. Polly looked up sharply.

'Ain`t got time to do that, girl. There's the chamber pots to empty and the fires to light, yet.'

'Don't worry,' said Rachel and she pulled herself together. 'I'll be fine, thanks.'

The day wore on and more fears came into Rachel's mind. Charles had talked of escape but how would he manage it? It was a dangerous business, she knew, and some prisoners had been shot by the militia whilst attempting it. She hated to think of him being hurt. If he did get away, how would they meet up and where would they go? So many questions. If only Rose had still been there to offer her usual sensible advice. She had always made Rachel see things more clearly. What was it she had said? *Do what your heart tells you to do.* Well, she thought, I will. I must. My heart tells me to go with Charles. He is the only person who has ever made me truly happy. I will take this chance and damn the consequences! Having made her decision, she felt immediately better. Her mind was at peace now. She still felt fearful but was fixed on her purpose. All doubts fell away.

On the other side of Peterborough Charles had spent the last two days in torment. What would Rachel decide? She had seemed so shocked by the idea. He wished he knew what she was thinking. If she said no, he felt he would die. He could not take this prison anymore, but to leave without her was not an option. As it was his week on the stall at least he was outside each day, but he was constantly watching out for Rachel. Surely, she would return that week. She had to! In the meantime, he occupied himself with finding out about the various escape attempts. He had to be very discreet in order to evade suspicion, so he made casual conversation with various inmates. It seemed the authorities were keen to hush up any successful escapes, but happy to loudly proclaim all the failures and recaptures. All the same, Charles heard many stories. There were those who had tried tunnelling or breaking down the perimeter, then there were those who had tried to impersonate the militia and slide out without being noticed. One man had even hidden in the night soil cart and been taken out that way, though he nearly suffocated in the attempt! Certainly, there was talk that the guards could be bribed to *look the other way*, though they were not to be trusted. Several who had taken the pay off, had then turned in the unfortunate individuals in order to claim a reward! The easiest method seemed to be to get a forged pass and simply walk out of the gate, pretending to be a civilian labourer returning home. But Charles had not yet found out who was the mastermind behind the forged passes. However, he did know that a couple of years earlier, there had been a racket in forging bank notes until those involved had been caught. One of them, Francois Raige, was still at Norman Cross and Charles was determined to ask him. After all, if he could forge bank notes, then surely a pass would be child's play to him? Charles just needed to find him, which was easier said than done. Then there was the small matter of getting hold of suitable clothing. The bright yellow prison suits rather tended to stand out, and certainly would not aid escape. Still there were inmates who had been tailors in their previous lives and Charles was sure something could be arranged. He had money after all from the sale of his carved goods, and money had been known to smooth many a bumpy path in its time.

It was the end of the week before Rachel was free to visit again. Though she had gone over everything in her head many times, she always reached the same conclusion. If that is what her lover wanted to do, she would go with him. It was worth the risk.

Charles was nervous when he saw her approaching, wondering what her decision would be. A guard was standing close by the stall, so they could say nothing personal. Rachel pretended to be a customer and picked up a carved ship. She smiled at Charles trying to convey how she felt without saying it.

'Have you made a decision, Mam'selle, on the ship I mean?'

Charles asked.

'Oh yes, I have. The answer is yes! I definitely want that.' She gazed into his eyes, smiling.

'Are you sure?' he asked. 'You have no doubts?'

'None whatsoever!' she declared. 'Let me pay you for it.'

Handing over the money their hands touched briefly. The guard moved off to the next stall and they gained a few precious moments to themselves.

'Cherie,' whispered Charles, 'I am so glad. Come and talk to me at the wall next week and we can make some plans.'

'Be very careful, my love,' Rachel said in a low voice. 'Don't take any risks. I will start getting ready at my end.'

'You have no regrets?' asked Charles.

'None,' she whispered. 'Now I must go or that fellow will get suspicious. See you next week.'

The guard was returning along the row of stalls.

'Well, thank you very much,' said Rachel in her normal voice. 'I'm sure this is exactly what I want.'

'You are most welcome, Mam'selle,' replied Charles. 'I hope we can do business again.'

They parted, their hearts full of hope and love. Maybe they would find their happiness. Why not take the chance and try?

Chapter 20

Charles hesitated to tell Johannes about his plans. He knew the jovial Dutchman would counsel him against anything so rash. His friend was a naturally cautious and sensible man. There were few people's opinions about whom Charles really cared, but he hated the idea of upsetting Johannes. What would his friend think when he found him gone, one day? Would he be hurt that Charles hadn't taken him into his confidence, or just wonder if he was well? As it was, Charles needn't have worried, for Johannes came to him a couple of days later with some surprising news. His eyes shining with happiness, Johannes announced:

'I'm going home! Me, my wife, little Henrik – we're all going. My turn of exchange has come up at last!'

'How wonderful for you,' said Charles. He was truly happy for his friend but would miss him, he knew.

'There are 100 Dutchmen being exchanged for Englishers next week,' Johannes continued. 'I can't believe it. It's almost too good to be true.'

'You deserve it,' Charles told him. 'It will be lovely for you and Maria to have a normal life again.'

Johannes burbled away happily about his plans for the future, how he wanted a farm and lots more children. Then he suddenly stopped and looked at Charles.

'I am so sorry,' he said. 'I am being thoughtless. You must hate me for it.'

'Not at all,' replied Charles. 'I am very happy for you.'

'You will be free one day as well,' said Johannes. 'This war cannot go on forever.'

'Yes,' said Charles. 'I think I will be free again soon. Do not worry about me. Enjoy yourself.'

He patted his friend on the back and left. Oh, how he would miss this dear kind man, but he had his own plans which would have meant goodbye in any case.

Now to find Francois Raige – that was the next task.

It was a few days before he accomplished this, finally finding the man mending hammocks, a job which occupied many. Charles had been warned not to trust him, as he had turned informer on his previous forgery colleagues, in order to save his own skin. Francois was a taciturn and grim-faced individual who growled at Charles:

'What?'

Careful not to let others overhear, Charles started to enquire whether he ever did any 'artwork' for people anymore.

'Don't know what you mean,' the man said, scowling.

'Engravings,' whispered Charles, 'documents, that sort of thing.'

'Given it all up, ain't you heard?'

Charles clinked a handful of coins in his pocket, discreetly.

'What about passes? Are you sure?'

Charles took out and fingered the money as if he was just

restless, but it caught Francois' attention.

'Well now, maybe as a special favour, perhaps,' he said. 'Just to keep me hand in. What you after?'

Charles explained quietly. Francois listened. Finally, he looked at the money in Charles' palm and said:

'Cost you double that, Le Boucher. Yes, I know your name, don't ask me how! If you can find the dosh then I'll do it, and I'll take that as a down payment.' He grabbed the coins from Charles before he could stop him and pocketed them.

'Come back in three days and bring the rest of the cash.'

Then Francois turned back to his work, leaving Charles to ponder whether he would ever see anything for his money.

'How do I know…' he began. Francois glared.

'Just have to trust me, won't you?' he jeered.

Feeling faintly dissatisfied Charles left, unaware that he was being watched by a small, weaselly faced man who went scampering off to report his findings to an interested party.

At the vicarage, Rachel was pondering on her belongings. They were meagre enough, it was true, but it was clear that when they fled, she wouldn't be able to take them all. They would need to travel fast and light. Reluctantly she pulled out everything she thought she wouldn't need. Her lovely dress that was bought for the dance would have to go. It just wasn't practical. No, she needed warm, hard-wearing clothes for country life. She could always buy more things later, she reasoned. Sadly, she hung the dress up in the cupboard, and determined not to look at it again. A few family mementoes lingered in her travel bag – she just couldn't bear to leave them behind. They were part of her past life which she was about to abandon forever, but still she clung

173

to them. If only her family would accept her relationship, she thought, but even if they did, they wouldn't understand this.

Charles meanwhile was dealing with a sadness of his own. It was the day of Johannes' departure and he felt it keenly. His friend was smiling proudly as he came say goodbye. Wearing his old uniform (tattered though it was), Johannes suddenly seemed to have grown in stature. He was no longer a prisoner, but a free man again, on his way back to his native land. With him was his wife Maria and his young son. They all shook hands joyfully, but Charles was feeling choked with emotion. He wished Johannes well, his words seeming inadequate for the occasion.

'Take care, my friend,' said Johannes. 'Don't worry, you'll be out of here soon enough, I'm sure.'

Thinking to himself that this was surely true, Charles managed a wry smile. On a sudden impulse he enveloped Johannes in a big bear hug, then, wiping eyes that were suspiciously moist, with his sleeve, he said cheerfully:

All the best, mon ami. Bon voyage and bon chance. Now be off with you!'

They laughed and parted, waving as they went. The waiting cart was full of equally happy inmates, all impatient for their freedom at last. Charles watched as they moved off, through the huge perimeter gates into the wide world beyond. One day soon, he thought, it will be my turn, but not like this. No, I have my own way.

The next problem Charles faced was finding suitable clothing in order to leave the camp, unnoticed. There were several ex-tailors in the laundry department but when he asked them if they could make civilian style clothes, they shook their heads.

'More's the pity, no,' said Alexandre, who was Charles' best hope. 'Just can't get the cloth you see. It's all that darned yellow colour!'

'Could you dye it?' asked Charles.

'Maybe, but it's risky. Too many guards around all the time. Last time someone managed to get out incognito, they stole a guard's uniform, but they're locked up tight now. No chance!'

Charles sighed. There must be some way. He watched and he waited.

Three days went by, and Charles returned to Francois for the pass. He'd managed to collect the money that the forger had demanded and was hopeful that he would receive his purchase. However, when he asked Francois for his goods the inmate just laughed.

'I have the money you asked for,' Charles told him. 'I've kept my end of the bargain. Now where is it?'

'In a safe place, my friend,' Francois replied smoothly, 'but there it will stay until you find me more.' Then he named a figure that was double what he had originally requested. Charles gasped.

'Why? That's not fair!'

'Take it or leave it!' said Francois. 'I've heard you're dead keen to leave. If you don't like it, find someone else!'

He laughed again and Charles left feeling angry and desperate. This would take every penny he had and leave him with nothing. How could he hope to get clothing without some funds? Maybe Rachel could help.

Charles was back on the inside of the perimeter wall again, the next time his beloved visited. They knew this would be so, but it was hard after having seen each other face to face recently. They were both cautious in the conversations.

'How are things going with you?' asked Rachel. 'Have you made any progress?'

'Yes and no,' answered Charles. 'There are delays and problems.' He paused. 'I hate to ask but have you any money? There are some materials that I need for my task which are costing more than I expected.'

Rachel opened her purse and pulled out all the coins she had. She waited until the guard had passed out of sight again, then handed them up to Charles through the hole in the wall.

'It's all I have on me at the moment,' she whispered, 'but I can get more.'

'Bless you, my cherie. I will use it wisely, never fear. I love you.'

'Take care, my love,' she said.

Returning to Francois the next day, Charles was determined to get the pass. This time he took the knife he used for carving the ornaments out of bone. It was small and sharp, and Charles hoped to frighten the double-crossing forger into giving him his dues.

Francois was alone in his barracks when Charles entered.

'Oh, you,' he said with a sneer, 'have you got what I asked for?'

'Yes,' replied Charles calmly. 'Here.'

He handed Francois the amount the inmate had demanded last time.

'Hmm, well let me see. There's been a lot more labour and time spent on this than I expected, and it's been very risky. I'm sure someone else would pay very well for it. Maybe I should charge more.'

Charles had had enough. He grabbed Francois by the collar and drew his knife.

'You're a double-crossing rogue, Monsieur Raige! I will have what you agreed to do, at the price we agreed. This is all I have and there won't be any more. Do you understand me?'

The knife glinted in the dusty sunlight that trickled through the windows and Francois quailed.

'Yes, yes, of course. I was just thinking aloud, that's all. Of course, you can have it. Here!'

He thrust the document at Charles who released him and studied it. It seemed satisfactory. In disgust, Charles flung the money at Francois and walked off clutching the hard-won pass. At least one part had been achieved. Now for the clothing.

Rachel returned with more money the following week. A few days earlier she had pulled out all her savings from the little chest she kept under the bed and had counted up. There was quite a bit there, she was pleased to find. Of course, people working in domestic service had little chance to spend their income, their lives being mostly dictated by their employers. Being in charge of the household Rachel was freer than most in this respect, but she needed little. Food and lodging were all found for her as part of her employment, so she had been able to save.

When she went into town, she enquired the price of tickets at the stagecoach office.

'Where to, Ma'am?' asked the clerk.

'Where is the farthest you go?' Rachel replied.

'We go all over, Ma'am. Don't you know where you want to go?'

'Well, no, not yet' said Rachel blushing. 'I'm still thinking about it.'

'London's probably the farthest, Ma'am. Depends what direction you want. We also go north and east.'

Rachel made a note of prices and departure times and left feeling embarrassed. She felt as if she was acting suspiciously but knew that the man couldn't possibly guess what they were up to. Now that she knew the prices, she carefully put away two full fares plus some extra for provisions then went to see Charles.

Her lover had been busy in the past few days chatting to some of the civilian labourers who worked at the depot. Some didn't want to talk, but one seemed a decent enough fellow and Charles had managed to get quite friendly. The man's name was Samuel, he was married, Charles found out, and had five hungry children.

'This 'ere work's all that keeps us from the poor house,' the labourer told him. 'Me missus, Martha that is, takes in washing and the like but with all them kids to feed it's mighty hard to get by.'

This was exactly what Charles wanted to hear. An impoverished family would be glad of more cash and Charles knew just what he could offer them - a substantial payment in return for some civilian clothes. However, he decided to take things slowly. No good rushing. After all he didn't know the man that well yet. Maybe he couldn't be trusted, or worse, couldn't be bribed. Perhaps he was one of those rare things – an honest man. Well, time would tell.

'I've been getting on with that new project I told you about,' he said to Rachel when they next met.

'The first part is complete now, and the next part shouldn't take that long. I'll let you know how it goes and when to expect delivery.'

Rachel trembled as she passed Charles the money. The idea of actually carrying out their plan was terrifying and yet exciting at the same time. The closer they got to it, the more she worried that something would go wrong. Whilst in the market the other day she'd heard a stallholder say:

'Did you hear? Another one of those prisoners tried to escape from the camp last week. Shot him, they say as he was trying to get over the wall. Serves 'im right!'

It's true there had been another failed escape attempt the week before, which had made Charles think twice, but there was no going back now, he told himself. This was something he had to do.

The project progressed a couple of days later when Charles saw Samuel again. The labourer looked very depressed.

'How are you?' asked Charles. 'You look very sad, my friend.'

Samuel sighed. 'Me eldest was fair poorly so we had to call the physic, but now we can't pay the bill. And then the landlord is after 'is money and we ain't got it. I don't know what to do!'

Charles sympathised. 'What you need is some extra cash,' he said. 'Maybe I could help if you could do a little something for me.'

The man looked up. 'Really?' he said his eyes alight with hope in his despair. 'But what could I do for you?'

Charles took him by the arm and led him away into a quiet corner.

'I need some clothes,' he told him. 'Something less colourful, if you get what I mean.'

Samuel stared in shock at Charles. 'Why? I mean – what you gonna do? Something stupid, perhaps?'

'Perhaps,' replied Charles, 'but don't worry it won't be traced to you. If you help me, then I can help you.'

He showed Samuel the coins he had in his pocket and the man's eyes widened.

'Well, I dunno. I'm not sure I should.'

'But you could sort out all your problems,' said Charles persuasively, 'all in return for just a few old clothes, the older the better in fact.'

Samuel was reluctantly convinced. A desperate man has few options, after all. Next day he returned to the depot wearing extra layers of clothing which he dutifully gave to Charles. There were trousers, a shirt, an old coat and a hat. All suitably shabby and dirty.

'I didn't tell Martha nothing,' Samuel said. 'She wouldn't approve.'

He hesitated as he took the money.

'Please be careful,' he said. 'I feel you're a decent man, about to do a foolish thing. 'Ere, I brought you a few extras, just in case.'

He handed Charles a cloth bag which he discovered later had a hunk of bread, some apples and a small bottle of a mysterious brown liquid. They shook hands and Samuel went on his way, leaving Charles feeling humbled by the poor man's kindness.

'Well,' he said to himself, 'that's it now. We're all ready to go.'

The thought made him tremble inside.

Chapter 21

It was a fine summers evening in June and Rachel was standing by the side of the turnpike road, clutching her bag and looking nervously about her. This was where the stagecoach stopped on its way up north to Lincoln and beyond, but the coach arrived punctually at 6 o' clock, and Rachel didn't get on. The driver was very annoyed that she'd booked two spaces, which she now didn't seem to want.

'What you book them for, then?' he demanded. 'Ain't you going? You're here, ain't you?'

She couldn't explain, but with a heavy heart watched the coach roll off into the distance without her. Hours went by and she was still waiting, getting increasingly anxious. What had happened? Where was Charles? In her heart she knew something had gone wrong. Sadly, she returned to the vicarage.

They'd planned it all the week before, deciding it was best to leave on Rachel's day off. That way her absence wouldn't be noticed until 9 o' clock when she failed to return to her duties. Rachel debated whether to leave a note, so as to alleviate people's fears about her, but thought if she left it somewhere visible then it might be discovered before she wanted her departure to be known. After much consideration she wrote one and left it in the cupboard. That way, if anyone looked to see if she had taken her clothes, they would find it. Rachel hated to think of people worrying about her. Now she sat in her lonely room and tore the note into tiny shreds. She had a feeling they weren't going anywhere.

It was a simple enough plan. All Charles had to do was to don the labourer's clothes, take his pass and walk out the gate, past the guards, hopefully unnoticed. He hadn't bargained for Black Jemmy, however. The spies had been out and about and had reported back.

In a dark corner of the barracks Charles dressed quietly and hastily in the old clothes that Samuel had sold him. Pushing his camp uniform into a bin and pulling the hat down tightly to disguise his face, he started a slow saunter towards the gate. Not too fast, he told himself. Casual now, as if it's normal. His heart was beating fast, and his hands were sweating. In his pocket he had the pass, what little was left of his money and (though he didn't really know why) his small knife.

He wandered slowly towards the perimeter, each step seeming to take an age. Out of the corner of his eye he saw a movement and was horrified to see Jemmy approaching. Trying to pretend he hadn't noticed he continued walking but quickened his pace slightly. All of a sudden however, there was a shout.

'Le Boucher! I see you. What you up to? 'Ere, Mr Halliday, Sir! I think something's going on.'

Charles panicked. He started to run towards the gate, but Jemmy was on him in a flash, clutching at his clothes and knocking off his hat. Charles' identity was revealed for all to see. It was no use. All he could do was to turn and fight. They grappled in an ugly tangle of legs and arms. Jemmy's fingers scratched Charles' face and tore at his clothes. But then Charles managed to land a punch on his assailant's cheek which sent the man down. Too late! The alarm had been raised. Charles heard shouts all around him. Desperate, he turned and headed away from the man sprawled on the ground. He stumbled on but was headed off by another of his foes – Halliday. The warden had a vicious smile on his face and a large cudgel in his hand. He swung it at Charles, and it caught him on the side of his head, stunning him. They tumbled to the ground, struggling and cursing but Halliday had the better of him and rained blows down on Charles with the stick, until he couldn't take any more. Covering his head with his hands, Charles found a last desperate strength that he didn't know he had. How it happened Charles could never say, but suddenly Halliday lay there bleeding and moaning with a gash in his side, and Charles' knife was in his hands, glistening red. For a moment, he stared at it in disbelief. At that minute he was seized by several guards with rifles and promptly removed to the black hole, taking many a beating along the way. It was all over, and Charles knew that this time there would be no reprieve. In the darkness his physical pain meant nothing to him, besides the loss of the beautiful dream that they had had. Now there would be no new life with Rachel; in fact, he doubted whether he would ever see her again. How stupid he had been, he told himself, and he wept bitterly.

Governor Pressland sighed as he listened to the whole sorry tale the next morning. Another escape attempt and this time a warder nearly killed. Miraculously, Halliday, though badly injured, was alive and recovering in the hospital. The governor ordered Charles to be brought to him for questioning.

'Well?' Pressland demanded. 'What have you got to say for yourself?'

Charles was downcast and ashamed as he hung his head and mumbled:

'I'm sorry, Sir.'

'Sorry! That won't make things right, you know. You nearly killed a man!'

Charles looked up. 'Nearly? Then he's alright? Thank goodness! I never meant to hurt anybody, Sir.'

Pressland scanned Charles' face intently and could see that he was truly remorseful. He softened slightly.

'Tell me why you did this,' he said. 'It may make a difference.'

Charles hesitated to explain his love for Rachel, as relationships with civilians were officially frowned upon. Everyone knew it went on, but the authorities could not be seen to condone it.

So instead, he stammered:

'The walls – they close me in. I am suffocating here. I cannot take it anymore!'

Pressland listened and couldn't help feeling partly responsible. Maybe he had forced this man to act so desperately by cancelling his parole? But then he had to consider the seriousness of the injury and the violence, and he knew he couldn't afford to be lenient. Even so, he wanted to give him another chance.

'Another thing,' the governor asked, 'where did you get those clothes and that pass? Tell me and we may be able to consider your offence in a more charitable manner.'

Charles thought briefly about telling on Francois. After all the man was a rogue who hadn't thought twice about squealing on his own colleagues. But then Charles considered that if he told on Francois, he would also have to betray Samuel and that was something he would never do. The labourer was a decent man who, he, Charles, had led astray. He could not let him down. Civilians who helped prisoners escape were always severely punished. He shook his head:

'Non, non, I cannot.'

184

'I admire your loyalty,' said Pressland, 'but it is misplaced. This stubbornness will not help your case.'

'So be it,' replied Charles. 'I am not a snitch.'

'Well, it'll be the Chatham hulks for you, no doubt, but first I will have to send this all up the board to decide. It is a very serious matter.'

'Yes Sir', muttered Charles. He was taken back to the black hole again, but this time he had a glimmer of hope. After all, Halliday was going to be alright; surely that would help.

Pressland consulted the board the next day but was shocked by their decision. Their solicitor was adamant.

'This man is a villain, and must stand trial, Governor. We cannot afford to mollycoddle him. We must make an example of him. He is a dangerous rogue.'

'In his defence,' said Pressland timidly, 'he has never been like this before.'

'So, he is a model prisoner then?'

'Well, no, there have been a few incidents,' admitted the governor, remembering Halliday's reports, 'but nothing violent, just insubordination.'

'It is clear he was just working up to this murderous attack. He must stand trial in the court assizes. You are to send him to Huntingdon Gaol and await the outcome. The local newspaper has already got hold of this story and if we don't do something quickly, they will spread stories about us treating the enemy too gently. Public opinion is dead against them, you know. There would be an outcry if we let this go. No, he must have a full public trial. It's the only way.'

Pressland sighed, but he knew when he was beaten.

As the cart rattled away bearing Charles to Huntingdon Gaol, Rachel meanwhile was busy finding out the local gossip in the vicarage kitchen.

'Did you hear? One of them Frenchies stabbed a warden up at the prison camp!' said Polly, who always seemed to know everything.

'Terrible,' said Kitty with a shudder. 'What happened?'

Rachel paused in her work, listening, a feeling of dread in her stomach. Surely not?

'E tried to escape and ran into Mr Halliday; you know that chap who lives in the lodge up at the camp? Murderous, 'e was! Tried to kill him, they say. Nearly managed it too, but the guards arrested him. I hear they're sending him off the hulks.'

Rachel flushed as she asked as casually as she could:

'Do you know what the prisoner's name was?'

'Oh, er, Butcher or somethin' like that. You alright, Ma'am? You gone quite pale.'

'Just need some air,' Rachel replied and moved swiftly outside. She felt faint with horror. Now what? What would they do to Charles? She had to find out.

Determined to go to the prison depot and ask, Rachel hurried off into town. But she didn't need to go to Norman Cross after all, for it was all around the market square. The headlines shouted:

'Attempted murder of prison warden! Turnkey's lucky escape! Prisoner sent to Huntingdon Gaol for trial.'

Rachel could hardly believe her ears. Trial! What would they decide? How could she see her lover if he was in gaol? Oh, how dreadful. She no longer knew what to think. Their dreams were in tatters.

Chapter 22

Huntingdon County Gaol loomed conspicuously over the town, situated as it was, near the High Street. Its gloomy and forbidding exterior gave an impression of importance, which the actual capacity belied. It could take just ten inmates at any one time and half of those were usually debtors, rather than felons. Charles knew he came into the latter category and would be treated accordingly. It was only three or four weeks before he became weak from lack of proper nourishment, poor sanitation and ill treatment. The warders delighted in, and were encouraged to administer beatings on a regular basis. There was no-one to complain to here, no rights and no leniency. He was a felon and could expect nothing else. Charles realised, all too late, that Norman Cross was a palace compared to this. In his heart he knew this was all he deserved, and he cursed his moment of foolishness. Halliday had been the bane of his life and it seemed he still was.

Clinging bravely to the outside seat of a stagecoach and praying she wouldn't fall off; Rachel wished the vehicle would go faster. The beauties of the great fenland they passed through were totally lost on her at that moment, though as a rule she appreciated the joys of the countryside. The roads however were so badly rutted that the coach tumbled about all over the place, shaking every bone in her body. The season was dry and warm, so at least she wasn't getting wet in her exposed position, but clouds of choking dust flew up making her cough and splutter. Progress from Peterborough to Huntingdon was unbearably slow and uncomfortable. Normally Rachel would only have considered travelling inside the stagecoach, but having spent most of her money on two tickets which were never used, all she had left was enough to pay for the cheapest of seats.

Hours later, Rachel climbed down thankfully but painfully, stiff and aching in every limb. Looking around her at the town she felt suddenly unsure and nervous. What was she doing here? she asked herself. What could she possibly hope to achieve? She didn't even know if they allowed visitors to the jail, but she knew she had to try. She felt that she must see Charles. These last few weeks had been torture for her.

Huntingdon seemed a pleasant enough town, she considered. The Great Ouse flowed tranquilly through the centre and under an ancient bridge, which she could only admire. But her heart was elsewhere and after obtaining directions at The George coaching inn, where she alighted, she headed off to the gaol.

It took every bit of Rachel's courage to present herself at the imposing gate to the prison and ask to be admitted. A stern guard frowned at her as she explained she wanted to visit an inmate.

'Not done, normally,' he said. 'What you want to do that for? I'll have to ask the guvnor.'

'Please do that,' replied Rachel in a voice more confident than she felt. 'I'll wait.'

The governor duly arrived and gave her a grilling about her reasons for the visit.

'Madam, are you aware that these are dangerous felons? Are you sure that this is what you want? This man – Le Boucher – is an attempted murderer you know. I can't be held responsible for your safety whilst you're here.'

'Charles would never hurt me,' declared Rachel. 'I insist on seeing him. Surely, I have my rights.'

'On your own head be it,' grunted the governor. 'Guard, take her to the day room and fetch Le Boucher. Ten minutes maximum, however.'

'Ten minutes?' cried Rachel. 'But I've come a long way!'

'It's that or nothing. Take yer choice. What's more you'll have to be searched.'

Rachel reluctantly submitted to all their demands. All she had brought for Charles were some apples and nuts, guessing that anything else was likely to be confiscated. The guard studied them suspiciously but let them pass. Then finally she was led into the body of the jail. She was escorted to a bleak, square dayroom which shocked her by its small size and cramped conditions. A trap door in the floor led down some steps into a dark hole below, the purpose of which Rachel shuddered to think. Three or four rough looking fellows were gathered in the bare room, mostly sitting on low benches. One man stood gazing wistfully out of the small, iron barred window and she realised with a start that it was Charles.

'Le Boucher!' the guard snarled. 'Here's a visitor for you.' Charles turned, surprised and his face showed dismay when he saw Rachel. He came forward unsteadily on weak legs, looking grey and haggard.

'Rachel - here? You! Really?' he managed.

He held out his hands and she grasped them eagerly.

'You two can go in there,' the guard told them indicating a

190

smaller side room. 'It's quiet in there, but mind; you only got ten minutes. I'll be back shortly.'

He left them and they stared at each other, not able to say a word. In the smaller room it was equally bare and badly lit, but at least there was no-one else there.

'My love,' said Rachel, 'how are you?' The words seemed inadequate, but she couldn't think what to say. For answer all Charles did was to hold her, his head resting on her shoulder whilst he wept bitter tears. Rachel held him close and tried her best to soothe his pain.

Eventually Charles said: 'You shouldn't have come here. It's not a place for the likes of you. Oh, I'm so sorry, Rachel! It all went wrong. You know I'm not a violent man. I don't know how it happened. I'm sorry, forgive me.'

'There's nothing to forgive,' Rachel told him. 'We tried to follow our dream and it failed. It's not your fault. But oh, how I wish we'd never thought of it!'

They clung together, both overcome with emotion.

'I'll be tried here at the Michaelmas Assizes,' Charles said. 'The charge is attempted murder.'

'I'm sure they'll see you didn't mean it,' said Rachel, trying to reassure him. 'Then you'll be sent back to the camp.'

'Maybe,' Charles replied, 'but I think they want justice to be seen to be done. They've sent me here so that I can have a public trial. If I'm found guilty you know what that will mean, don't you?'

They both trembled at the thought. The usual punishment for murder was death by hanging. There was a silence.

'I'll vouch for your character,' said Rachel. 'I'm sure that would help.'

Charles smiled at her fondly. 'It's a nice thought, cherie, but I doubt you will be allowed.'

'Times up!' came the shout, as the guard returned.

'I'll visit again,' promised Rachel, clasping Charles to her in a desperate embrace. Then she was torn away from him, out of the dim room into the bright daylight of the town. As she left, she asked the guard the reason for the trap door.

'That, Miss, leads into their sleeping quarters. Three beds down there, three men in each.'

'That's awful!' exclaimed Rachel. 'Three in a bed! What do they sleep on?'

'Straw and sacking, of course,' snorted the guard.' What did you expect – feather beds?' He erupted with laughter at her expense. 'Them's villains, Miss. Rogues the lot of 'em. Sorry if that offends you, you being 'intimate' with one, so to speak, but it's the honest truth!'

Rachel asked no more questions of her escort and was glad to escape into the outside world again. The prison was a place of despair and oppression and her spirits felt crushed. Walking around the town her mood lightened a little, looking at the bustling shops and the lively hostelries. A mass of people went about their business, each happy or sad in their own way, their lives mirrored in the waters of the Great Ouse. Sitting on a bench by the river Rachel saw her own reflection and gazed at it: a sad old woman she thought, but one in love nevertheless, and who was loved in return, in spite of everything. That made her smile and she felt better.

There was an hour to go before the long arduous stagecoach journey back to Peterborough, so Rachel decided to find some refreshment. She had risen early and barely breakfasted before her departure and suddenly she realised she was very hungry. There was a respectable looking pie shop near the marketplace, so she stopped and partook. Whilst she ate however, the local gossip flowed around her, and she was dismayed to hear talk of the prison.

'Did you hear, Eva, they hung that chap who stole those sheep the other day?'

'Really? Well, it's hard to go taking folks' livelihoods and all. Mind, `twasn`t like he was a murderer or something.'

'No. They reckon they've got a dangerous one in there now. Frenchie, he is, stabbed someone.'

'Shocking! He'll hang for sure, then.'

'Dead cert, I reckon. Serves 'im right!'

Rachel suddenly felt that she couldn't eat another thing, so she paid up hurriedly and left. She headed up Market Hill towards the stagecoach depot. Halfway up she was met by the sight of a large stately looking building labelled Town Hall and Assizes Court. So, this was it. This was where Charles' future would be decided. In spite of the elegant columns and impressive exterior Rachel hated it immediately. A cold, hard hearted building, she decided, ready to dispense justice (and punishment) to the people without a single ounce of compassion.

It was several weary hours later when Rachel finally made it back to the vicarage. Tired out, she went up to her housekeeper's room. There was just half an hour before she was due to return to her duties. No sooner had she got there, however but Kitty knocked on the door.

'Letter for you, Mrs Alderman,' said the maid. 'Came this morning. I hope it's not bad news or nothin.'

Rachel rarely received letters so was somewhat surprised. Thank goodness dear Rose had taught her to read, she thought. After Kitty had gone, she opened it. It was from her niece Sarah and was brief and to the point:

Dear Aunt

It may interest you to know that my long-lost brother James, believed dead for some time, has been found and is returned to us safely. He has been a prisoner of war in France and has just been exchanged for a prisoner from Norman Cross in order to get him home. We are of course delighted. We have however told him of your regrettable liaison with the enemy and he has expressed a desire that you do not visit him at this moment. I am sure you will understand and comply with his wishes.

Yours sincerely

Sarah.

James? Home? How wonderful. And yet how unfortunate that her family still felt like this and wouldn't let her see him. She didn't know whether to be happy or sad. What a day, she thought and with that she got ready for work. Life must go on, she told herself firmly.

The more Rachel thought about her family, when she finally had time to take a breath, the more she felt she must try and see them. Thinking about James being home encouraged a glimmer of hope. Surely, he wasn't the one who was denying her any contact. He'd been a soldier himself and would hopefully understand her point of view. Perhaps the letter would allow her a way back in, after all, it was the first time she'd heard from them in many weeks. Having convinced herself that this was a good sign she decided that she would visit. Hopefully, they wouldn't turn her away. She needed them so much at the moment.

A couple of days later, on her half day off, Rachel dressed carefully and set out to Sarah's house. Stopping at a shop on the way, she purchased some fresh baked cakes as a gift (a peace offering, she thought). She knocked nervously on the front door and was pleased to see James come to answer it. He looked tired and worn and leaned heavily on a cane.

'Aunt Rachel,' he said, surprised. 'What are you doing here?'

'Dear James, I am so pleased to hear you made it home!' Rachel moved to embrace him, but he shrank away from her.

'No, don't!' he said in a strange voice. 'I hear you have been consorting with the enemy, whilst I have been stuck in one of their prison camps!'

'James,' said Rachel, 'you must understand, surely? Charles was just a soldier like yourself, doing his duty.'

'Hah!' her nephew snorted. 'Don't give me that. They're barbarians! How could you?'

'Please,' pleaded Rachel, 'I just want to be part of the family again.'

'That can never be,' said James. 'You are a stranger to us now. Please leave.'

The door shut firmly in Rachel's face, and she turned away in tears. Even so, she could not regret her involvement with Charles. Their love was the one shining light of her whole life, no matter what the future might bring. Halfway home she realised that she still had the cakes, so on impulse she gave them to one of the beggars in the street. It was an old woman, dirty and dressed in rags, who was pathetically grateful.

'Bless you, dearie, you're an angel,' she said, noticing that Rachel had been crying. 'May the good lord soothe your troubled soul.'

This made Rachel remember that she still had much to be thankful for. There's always someone worse off than yourself, she thought and drying her eyes determinedly, she headed home to the vicarage.

Chapter 23

The sun was glaring out of a sullen sky and the storm clouds were gathering. August had been an unpredictable month so far; one moment dry and sunny, the next a deluge of rain. Today Rachel felt stifled in her heavy housekeeper's uniform and wished she could change into something cooler, but appearances had to be kept up at all times.

'Missus Alderman,' Kitty called as she came back downstairs from serving the afternoon tea, 'the Reverend says you're to come upstairs and see him at once, and to my mind he don't sound too happy.'

Rachel frowned. 'Please don't speculate about the master, Kitty. It isn't proper.'

'Well take care of yerself, Ma'am, that's all I say.'

Rachel wasn't unduly worried as she went to see Reverend Tutte. She knew she always did her best for the household, in spite of her personal troubles, and had no qualms about her work.

To her surprise however, her master did indeed look annoyed.

'Mrs Alderman,' he began, 'I have received a very serious complaint about you, which I feel I must address.'

'A complaint?' Rachel said, confused.

'Yes. My beloved sister Letitia has a housekeeper, who you engaged on her behalf. This woman has now disappeared without notice and there is an amount of money missing. My sister tells me that you failed to get references for the woman and that therefore she holds you personally responsible for this disaster.'

'But Sir, I…' began Rachel.

'I have to say that I agree with my sister,' the parson said. 'Really, you should have known better. I am quite dismayed by your lack of judgement. How could you?'

'But Sir, Mrs Bennett hadn't been working, so how could she have any references? She'd been looking after her family. I trusted her and took her on good faith.'

'That kind of attitude is not good enough. These things need to be in place. This woman could have been a murderer or something!'

'I'm sorry, Sir,' muttered Rachel, realising that there was no way she could excuse her actions.

'Sorry isn't good enough,' said Reverend Tutte, sternly. 'My sister needs help with all this. You are to go to London immediately to sort out the mess you made. Kitty and Polly will have to hold the fort here until you return.'

'Immediately! But Sir, it is my day off on Thursday. I can't! I have something I have to do.'

Rachel had planned to visit Charles again and was desperate not to miss it. It was already Monday afternoon so there was no chance of her being back by Thursday.

'I'm sorry,' the parson said, 'but this is your duty. You must go. You can have a day off at another time.'

'But Sir, please,' begged Rachel. 'Can't I wait until after

Thursday?'

The vicar eyed her with a stony face.

'No Madam, you cannot,' he said severely. 'You will go to London tomorrow, or I will have to reconsider your position here. After all, this is your fault.'

Rachel was stunned. To think this was how she was being treated after all these years of service. Still, she couldn't afford to lose her job, so she hung her head and said meekly:

'Yes of course, Sir. I will go and get ready for London. Please accept my apologies for being so forthright. I don't know what came over me.'

The vicar softened slightly. 'Well, I'm glad you are seeing sense. You can have a day off when you get back.'

'Yes Sir,' she mumbled, then retreated downstairs.

The stagecoach rumbled slowly along the next day and Rachel had plenty of time to reflect. To think she had felt bad about the idea of leaving the vicarage behind when they had planned to flee! She'd been loyal to the Reverend, but it seems he didn't feel that way about her. Eight years she had worked there, with never a stain on her character, but in a second it counted for nothing. Did she regret engaging Mrs Bennett as a housekeeper without references? No. She would do the same again, she decided. People needed to be given a chance, even if sometimes that backfired.

The journey was faster than the previous time, Rachel was pleased to find, due to the increase in the number of turnpike gates which had improved the conditions of the roads. Hours later she was able to present herself to Mistress Letitia Holland. The vicar's sister had never been of an even temperament in any case, but today was worse than usual. She ranted and raged at Rachel in a very unseemly manner.

'It's all your fault. You will have to act as housekeeper for me until you find a suitable candidate to take your place, with references this time, mind! What's more the missing money will be stopped out of your pay.'

Rachel gasped but held her tongue. Finally, she was able to escape downstairs and find out the details of what had really happened. The butler, Thomas, was only too glad to talk.

'Mrs Alderman, if you don't mind me saying, I can't think too badly of Mrs Bennett. She's been doing a real fine job, and everyone likes her. I can't believe that she would take any money. She was always very strict about that.'

'Well,' sighed Rachel, 'you can never really tell what someone might be capable of, if they're pushed.'

'What do you mean?' said Thomas.

'Well, maybe she had personal troubles - family or something - that forced her into it. I wish we knew more.'

After sorting out the immediate household issues such as planning meals and organising laundry, Rachel also found time to talk to the other staff. Alice, the kitchen maid, seemed to think that Mrs Bennett had received a letter which caused her distress.

'I'm sure I saw that she'd been crying, Ma'am, just the day before she left.'

Looking over the housekeeper's room, Rachel discovered that not everything had been taken by her. Some clothes still hung in the cupboard, though her travel bag and outdoor shoes were missing. Maybe she had only intended to go for a short time, Rachel thought. No note had been left, explaining her absence, so they had been prompted to think the worst, but maybe this wasn't the case.

Then Rachel checked the household accounts and the cash box. It's true there was an amount not accounted for in the receipts - £11 and two shillings. Strange, mused Rachel, why would someone steal that amount? After all there was more cash left in the box. Surely, they would take whole pounds or guineas, unless it was for something specific perhaps.

Thursday arrived and Rachel couldn't help thinking about Charles and her missed appointment. How long would it be until she was able to get home, she wondered and redoubled her efforts to find a replacement.

Visiting a local employment agency, Rachel arranged for two suitable candidates to come for interview the next day. Then she went to the butchers to order the meat for the week. When she told the shop keeper who it was for, the man looked surprised.

'Oh, where's Mrs Bennett?' he asked. 'I was going to let her have this receipt from last month. I forgot to give it to her. It's for £11 and two shillings. I hope it hasn't caused her any worry.'

The missing money! So, it was never stolen at all. Rachel took the receipt and returned to the household, proudly bearing it with her. She went straight to Mrs Holland and told her the news.

'So, everything is accounted for Madam, and nothing is missing,' she concluded.

The mistress of the house did not look too impressed.

'Well, that's a relief, but I feel it's more by luck than judgement. She has left us totally in the lurch. Disgusting behaviour!'

Rachel told the rest of the staff, and they were glad to hear that Mrs Bennett had been cleared of theft.

'I knew she wasn't a bad lot,' said Alice. 'It's a real shame she's gone. Probably the mistress's fault anyway!'

'Hush!' said Rachel. 'No more talk like that, please.'

Privately she agreed but was unable to show it.

Friday morning came and so did the two applicants for the job. Rachel disliked both of them. One was a harsh snob, and the other a silly feeble woman who would never be able to control the staff of a busy London household. Mrs Holland, of course, preferred the former and so she was asked to start on Monday. Rachel felt for the existing staff, knowing that they would suffer from the change. Still at least it meant she would be able to return to Peterborough.

It was half past two when there was a knock on the kitchen door. Rachel heard a screech of delight as Alice opened it to find Mrs Bennett, the missing housekeeper, standing there.

'Mrs B's back!' called Alice. 'Come and see.'

The whole staff came running in, keen to welcome her back, but first Rachel had to find out what had been going on.

'Where have you been?' she demanded.

It turned out that Mrs Bennett had been called away suddenly to her grown up daughter who was dangerously ill. Unfortunately, she had not thought to leave a note in her anxiety to get to her.

'I am so sorry,' Mrs Bennett told her. 'I know I let everyone down but it's family and that comes first. There are three small children to be looked after as well, you see, but thank the Lord, my Emma's on the mend now.'

Rachel sympathised but knew the mistress wouldn't see it that way. She took the penitent housekeeper up to see Mrs Holland

and attempted to plead her case, but to no avail.

'Mrs Alderman, are you seriously asking me to trust this woman again? You must be joking. Who's to say that she won't do exactly the same another time? And you, Mrs Bennett - obviously you are not reliable. You are to leave this house immediately, and don't expect a reference!'

'Please Madam,' said Mrs Bennett, 'I can only beg your forgiveness. I meant to leave a note. It was an oversight for which I apologise.'

'I am not interested in your excuses!' Letitia cried. 'Get out! And you Mrs Alderman – get back to the countryside where you belong and think yourself lucky that I don't ask my brother to dismiss you for your lack of judgement!'

They fled from her presence. Taking refuge in the housekeeper's room the two of them commiserated with each other.

'I didn't mean to cause you any trouble,' said Mrs Bennett. 'I am sorry.'

'It's alright,' Rachel told her. 'I would have done the same. One thing I am going to do, and that is write a reference for you. It may not be quite as good as an employer's one, but it may help.'

Tears were shed as Mrs Bennett took leave of her staff. Rachel wished it could have been different, but it was not to be. The mistress was a vain and hard-hearted woman who cared little for her servants' welfare. They were just a necessity for daily living, nothing more.

A week later, Rachel was finally in the stagecoach on her way to visit Charles again. Her faith in her employer had been severely tested, but at least the parson had kept his word and given her a belated day off. It had been six weeks since she had last seen Charles, and although she was expecting a change in him, she was shocked by what she saw. He was thin and gaunt, his dark hair turning grey. He clutched at her, trying to hide in her loving arms. The vittles she had brought for him were eaten urgently, desperately, like a starving man, as indeed he was. The ten-minute visit brought neither of them much relief; and the pain of parting was worse than ever.

'Next time you visit will be the last,' whispered Charles. 'My trial is on the 29th of September, and I know what the result will be.'

'Don't talk like that, my love,' she replied. 'There is always hope. I will be there at the trial, watching and praying for you to be treated leniently. Don't despair.'

For answer all he could do was to cling to her, until once more she was wrenched away and sent outside.

Chapter 24

It was the 29th of September and Rachel dressed carefully, her fingers trembling as she did up the buttons of her best day dress. This was it, the day of reckoning, the day of the trial.

Only last week she had seen Charles and he had begged her to forget him. This time he was calmer and appeared resigned to his fate.

'I know what will happen to me, my love, and I feel I can bear it now.'

'But nothing is certain yet,' protested Rachel. 'You still have a chance.'

He smiled at her. 'Of course, cherie, but this will be our last time to talk. Whatever happens we will not be together again. You must forget about me.'

'Never!' declared Rachel, her eyes full of tears. 'You have given me so much.'

'Only pain, I fear,' said Charles, touching her cheek gently.

'No! That's wrong. You have changed my life for the better. Before, I was shy and lonely. I had never experienced anything in life. Now I have loved and been loved. It means everything to me. I have so many happy memories – our walks together, the dance, your kisses, our love. I cannot bear to lose you.'

'We will always be together in our hearts,' said Charles, 'even if it is in the afterlife. I will wait for you and one day we will be reunited with no more troubles to torment us, but I fear it will not be in this world.'

Rachel's tears poured down like rain.

'You must fight this charge,' she pleaded.

'I will do my best, cherie,' he promised. 'I am going to plead 'not guilty' in the hope of getting a lesser conviction. After all, I didn't mean to hurt him. But there are many witnesses who will say otherwise, unfortunately.'

'I will be there with you,' said Rachel. 'I promise.'

'I know,' said Charles and they kissed passionately. 'Dearest Rachel, you mean all the world to me,' he told her. 'I love you. Always remember that.'

'I love you too,' Rachel said. 'There will be no-one else, ever. You are the only one for me.'

The guard relented briefly and allowed them one last kiss before escorting Rachel from the cells. Once outside she asked to see the governor.

'How can I become a character witness for the trial?' she asked him.

The governor frowned. 'For him? Are you mad? Surely you know it's an open and shut case?'

Then he saw her face. 'Well now, it's nothing to do with me, anyway. You'll need to go to the courthouse and ask them there.'

Rachel went there next and asked a clerk who was on duty.

'A character witness? For a murderer? You must be joking!'

'I'm not,' insisted Rachel. 'Let me talk to someone about this.'

The clerk reluctantly called a court official who listened but gave her the same response.

'I'm sorry, Madam, but due to the seriousness of the case, we are not able to take character references for the accused. You do know there are many witnesses to this crime, don't you?'

'Yes!' cried Rachel. 'But he didn't mean to do it. Please let me speak up for him.'

'I'm sorry, Madam. That's the rule. No character witnesses for crimes of this nature. You can watch it from the public gallery if you like, then you'll know what happens.'

So here it was at last, the fateful day. Rachel had asked her master for an extra day off, but the request was denied.

'I'm sorry, Mrs Alderman, but you only had your day off just last week. Your next one is not due for three weeks. If I give you this,' Reverend Tutte told her, 'Everyone else will want the same.'

'Yes Sir,' mumbled Rachel, but there was no doubt in her mind that she would take it anyway. The night before the trial she told Kitty and Polly that she was feeling ill and retired early. Then the next morning, before she left, she wrote them a note saying she had gone to stay with her sister for a few days, because she had influenza. No matter what the consequences might be, she would be at the court with Charles. She had promised him.

The rain poured down, turning the roads into rivers of mud. Despite this, the stagecoach journey this time seemed to pass far too quickly as the dreaded hour approached. Time has sped up, she thought.

Sitting high up in the public gallery, Rachel watched and waited whilst several other unfortunate wretches were tried for various misdemeanours. Sentences were not passed at that time, they would be handed out at the end of the day, but verdicts were given, and many people were led away, weeping. Each case was over very quickly, barely lasting half an hour. There were twelve jurors, all keen to get through things as quickly as possible, and a judge who did most of the questioning. Finally, Charles was brought into the dock. Rachel held her breath.

'Le Boucher, you are accused of the attempted murder of warden Halliday at Norman Cross Prison camp. How do you plead?'

'Not guilty,' stated Charles.

'So be it. Call the first witness – Alexander Halliday.'

Charles was now face to face with his adversary for the first time since the incident. Halliday recounted the event in colourful and emotional language, even managing a tear or two, calling it 'a violent and pre-meditated attack.' The judge certainly appeared to be on the warden's side for he asked him at length about his pain and suffering, bringing out all the details for the jury to hear. Then the subject of Charles' character and general behaviour was raised.

'He was always a difficult and unpredictable prisoner, your honour,' said Halliday. 'I believe he was involved in the straw plait trade, which, as you know, is strictly against prison rules. When I tried to stop him, he was insolent and aggressive.'

'That's not true!' cried Charles.

'Silence!' ordered the judge. 'Tell me more, Warden.'

So, Halliday narrated various occasions, many of which had clearly been invented, when Charles was alleged to have been a dangerous individual. Charles was not allowed to respond to defend himself, the judge telling him he would get a chance later.

Then Governor Pressland was called to the stand. Charles was hopeful that the man might be more understanding, but unbeknownst to him, pressure had been applied by the prison board.

'We need a conviction on this, Governor,' they had told him. 'You understand, don't you? It's important for public confidence.'

Pressland conceded and obligingly toed the line. After all, his job was only given to him by the board, and it could easily be taken away. As his daughter had not long married the prison surgeon, he had the whole family to think of, so he did as he was told.

Following on from Halliday's accusations, the governor confirmed that Charles' reputation was a bad one and added that his parole had been cancelled due to his behaviour.

Other prison guards were also called as witnesses and they described the fight, each one making it sound more murderous than ever.

Finally, Charles took the stand and was interrogated without mercy by the judge and the accusers, until he could take no more.

'Please!' he shouted out. 'I didn't mean to hurt him. It was an accident.'

'An accident!' sneered the judge. 'Whilst trying to escape? I think not!'

The jury retreated briefly to consider their verdict, but it was unanimous. Guilty! Sentence would be passed later. Charles was taken away and Rachel sat there waiting, terrified to hear the worst.

Three hours later, sentencing started and eventually it was Charles' turn. He was brought up into the dock again, his head hung low, and his hands chained.

'Charles Le Boucher,' said the judge, 'you have been found guilty of cutting and maiming with intent to endanger life. I sentence you to be returned to Norman Cross Prison camp, where you will be hanged from the neck until you are dead. This will take place as soon as possible, in front of the inmates, to provide an example to any who may consider attempting a similar act.'

'No!' screamed out Rachel and she stood up in the gallery. 'No! He's a good man. Charles, I love you!'

Charles looked up and their eyes met briefly. He smiled, a special smile just for her. Then they took him away down the steps into the cells below. Rachel screamed again and at this point lost all self-control and started shouting at the officials of the court.

'It's not fair! He didn't mean to do it. Please listen. You can't do this!'

It was so unlike her normally, but she couldn't help it. The rest of the public stared at her and moved away. The door to the gallery opened and two uniformed men came in to 'escort' her out. She struggled with them but their hold on her was firm and unyielding, and very soon she found herself out on the street.

'Any more from you, missus, and you'll be up for disturbing the peace! So, stop yer wailing and go home!'

Rachel's anger was all spent. She collapsed onto the steps of the courthouse, all energy gone, tears running down her face. It was the end of her world.

Sometime later, Rachel came to again. An elderly man helped her up and kindly offered to buy her some tea, but she declined politely. First there was something she had to do. Bravely she went back into the court office to enquire what would happen next.

'Excuse me,' she stammered to the clerk, who eyed her suspiciously.

'Madam, if you're going to make a scene again, I will call the law and it'll be the worse for you, I warn you!'

'No, no, I'm sorry. I'm quite composed . Please can you just tell me how soon Charles Le Boucher will be sent back to Norman Cross for…. for…' (she couldn't say the words) '…for the punishment to be carried out?'

The clerk checked his books.

'Due to be transported back there late tomorrow, so it'll probably be the day after, or maybe even the day after that. It depends how long it takes to build the er…. well, you know what…' His voice tailed off, embarrassed.

'Thank you,' Rachel said. So, she had a day or two perhaps to get home and try and see him. She didn't know why but she felt she had to. The stagecoach had already left for the day, therefore the earliest she could get back to Peterborough was tomorrow. Sadly, she checked into a local hostelry, refusing their invitations to purchase food and drink. It would have choked her, she felt. Falling into bed, she curled into a ball and cried herself to sleep like a child.

Chapter 25

Arriving back at Peterborough the next day Rachel went straight to Norman Cross. She had to find out what was happening. The sentry on the gate could tell her nothing but he obligingly went and found a warden for her to talk to.

'Please Sir,' she pleaded, 'I am trying to find out what will happen about Charles Le Boucher, and when. Please help me.'

'Why do you need to know?' the warden asked. 'It's no business of yours, is it?'

'Yes! Yes, it is. He is my friend, and I would like to visit him.'

'Not much chance of that Missy. There won't be no visitors allowed. Besides sentence will be carried out the day after tomorrow.'

'Friday?' cried Rachel in anguish, 'but that's so soon. What time?'

'At sunrise, Miss. That's usual in these cases. Not that we've ever had it here before.'

'What time will he be back here?' she asked. 'Can I see him tomorrow?'

'Didn't I tell you? No visitors allowed!' the warden insisted, but then he looked thoughtfully at her. 'Well, maybe if you made it worth my while, I might be able to get you in,' he added. 'He'll be back this evening at 6 o' clock. If you can get hold of £10 by tomorrow, I'll see what I can do.'

'£10! But that's nearly a year's wages! I can't do that.'

'You can't want to see him that badly then,' the warden remarked sarcastically.

'Oh, but I do, please!'

'See what you can come up with then,' the man said. 'I'll be here tomorrow if you can find the money. That's the price.'

He walked back inside the camp leaving Rachel feeling distraught. She had no savings left now. How could she find that amount?

As she walked slowly back towards town her route took her near her sister Elizabeth's house and a thought struck her. The family were comfortably well off. Perhaps her sister would lend her the money. Knowing that Elizabeth shared Sarah's disgust at her behaviour made Rachel reluctant to approach her, but she had no other option.

Elizabeth opened the door to Rachel and in spite of herself, smiled in welcome. Though she agreed with Sarah in principle, Elizabeth had always felt very sad that Rachel had been rejected by the family.

'Rachel,' she said, 'what a surprise. Is anything amiss? You look unwell.'

She allowed Rachel into the parlour and they both sat there, feeling awkward.

Rachel couldn't think what to say now that she was there. The tears started again, and she murmured: 'I shouldn't have come. Forgive me.'

'Rachel,' said Elizabeth, 'you are still my sister, no matter what.

Are you in trouble?'

'Yes,' admitted Rachel, 'but I don't know how to say it.'

Elizabeth patted her hand kindly. 'Just tell me.'

Encouraged slightly, Rachel said: 'This is awful, I know. I hate to ask, but I need some money. Can you lend me any? I'm sorry. I have no-one else to turn to.'

'Oh, I see,' replied her sister, a little stiffly this time, moving her hand away. 'That's what it is. You're not 'with child' are you, from that man?'

'No!' cried Rachel, 'nothing like that, but I need £10 in order to get into the prison to see him. It's the last time I will ever be able to. He - he's being executed on Friday!'

Here Rachel started to sob, huge gasping sobs which shook her whole frame.

'Executed!' Elizabeth exclaimed, shocked. 'What for?'

Rachel couldn't talk for some time, racked with emotion. Her sister waited but made no effort to comfort her. Eventually Rachel explained as much as she was able.

'He had a fight with a warden and the man was hurt, but he didn't mean to do it. It was an accident!'

It was a limited version of the truth, but Rachel guessed that her sister wouldn't understand. She was right. Elizabeth's initial welcome for Rachel was fast fading away.

'I'm sorry,' said Elizabeth. 'I can't help you with this. For a start I don't have that kind of money, but even if I did, I couldn't let you have it, for this reason: you must know that if I did, I too would be rejected by the rest of the family, and I don't want that. I cannot be seen to condone your relationship with this man, I'm

214

afraid. If it was for something else, well maybe that would be different, though I doubt that Sarah would approve even then.'

Rachel stood up. 'I understand,' she said. 'I'll go. I shouldn't have asked you.' With that she walked to the door. Elizabeth followed.

'Rachel, I wish I could help you, but I just can't. Please believe me. Take care of yourself.' Her hand rested on Rachel's shoulder just for a moment and her eyes were moist with emotion.

'Goodbye,' said Rachel and left without looking back. She didn't blame her sister, but it was hard all the same. Just for a minute she'd thought that things might change, but no. That couldn't be. Life had taken them too far apart.

That night Rachel returned to her room at the vicarage. She had nowhere else to go. As she walked in through the back door she ran into Kitty and Polly in the kitchen.

'Mrs Alderman,' exclaimed Kitty, 'are you alright? We've been dead worried, me and Polly.'

'Yes,' said the cook. 'Got your note, but we kept it quiet, like.'

'Quiet?' queried Rachel.

'Well, we managed to cover for you,' Kitty explained, 'with the master, I mean. Told him you were busy at the market whenever he asked for you. Think we got away with it.'

'Thank you,' said Rachel with a sigh of relief. 'That's very good of you.'

'You still look ill, if you ask me,' said Polly in her usual blunt fashion. 'Go and get some rest.'

'I will do, thank you,' replied Rachel and retired to her room.

215

Seeing herself in the looking glass it was true she did look ill. Dark shadows under her eyes which were red and bloodshot, hair a mess, cheeks stained with tears – oh dear, what a state she was in, but she feared it would only get worse.

The next morning, however, Rachel did her best to bustle around the house as usual. If she stopped to think about anything she was in danger of going to pieces, so she kept busy and somehow got through. After lunch had been served, Rachel turned to the household accounts, all in order as usual. Just over £6 in the petty cash box; that would be such a help towards her cause to see Charles, she thought. Theft was not in Rachel's nature, but she was desperate. It would only be a loan anyway, she told herself. No-one would know. She could repay it later. Taking the cash plus her last tiny amount of savings she set off in the late afternoon, back to the depot to try and get in.

When the warden saw her again, he was pleased at first, until she told him how much money she had.

'I've got £6 and ten shillings. It's all I could raise. Please let me see Charles.'

He sneered at her. 'You must be joking! You know my price and I ain't budging.'

'Please,' she begged. 'I must see him.'

'What for?' the man said. 'There ain't no point. You got no future with him.' He laughed unpleasantly. '*He's* got no future at all! Now get lost.'

Rachel fled, defeated. Still at least she had time to return the 'borrowed' money without being labelled a thief. That was a relief. Putting it safely away in the cash box, she suddenly felt ashamed of herself. What could she have been thinking? How near had she come to being a criminal?

It was the last night before his sentence was due to be carried out and Charles sat in a single cell at Norman Cross, trying hard not to think about the next day. He focused on Rachel as much as he could and hoped that she would be well. He loved her as much as ever and although things hadn't turned out as he would have wished, he had no regrets about their relationship. His wife was a distant memory to him now and of no importance anymore. Rachel had been the love of his life, and if there was an afterlife, he thought, his only wish was to be reunited with her.

A kindly guard came with a special supper for him – tender meat cooked in the French way with sauce and herbs. Delicious, though Charles hardly noticed it. Later that evening the prison chaplain visited; a worthy man, serving all the different faiths of the camp, and trying to do his best. Charles was catholic, so the chaplain took his last confession and absolved Charles of all his sins. (If only it was as easy in real life, Charles thought to himself with a wry smile). Then they said Mass together, and the calm of the chanting and the flickering candlelight soothed him. He determined to die a good death on the morrow. Brave, strong, noble – that's what he hoped he would be, though truth to tell he was terrified.

The dreaded sunrise came, and Charles was escorted solemnly outside. Meanwhile Rachel had come to the outer prison walls. She felt she had to be there, despite the chill wind that blew right through her. From a little way back, on slightly raised ground, she could just see the top of the gallows that they had built the day before. Drums started to sound and there was a murmur of people gathered.

Charles walked out bravely to the waiting terror. Surrounding the platform was a huge crowd of fellow prisoners, all compelled to watch this punishment, by order of the authorities. Briefly he felt sorry for them. What a thing to have to see. Once up the steps onto the platform, Charles saw Halliday standing there, looking triumphant. He stopped and faced his opponent defiantly. Halliday sneered.

'Got what you deserve, Le Boucher, you rogue!'

Charles spat in his face.

'This is all you deserve,' he said, then he turned towards the hangman. 'Do your duty,' he told him.

The drums rolled louder as Rachel listened outside. Then there was the awful sound of a trap door opening followed by deadly silence and then a muted cheer. It was all over. Rachel could take no more and dropped in a faint to the ground. There she would have stayed had it not been for a kindly carter, delivering goods to the depot who found her and took her back to town. She came round as he lifted her onto the cart.

'Please leave me,' she muttered. 'I just want to die.'

'Oh no you don't Missy, not today. Now where do you live?'

Feebly she told him, and he delivered her safely back to the vicarage, where Kitty somehow managed to get her into bed. This time the Reverend had to be told that his housekeeper was not well. He was not best pleased but reluctantly sent for a doctor, who diagnosed nervous exhaustion and gave her a sedative.

'She needs to rest for several days,' he told them. 'I don't know what she's been doing but it hasn't done her any good at all. If she isn't better by the end of the week, she may have to go into a sanatorium.'

Through a haze of medication and emotional pain, Rachel heard but could not speak. As she sank into unconsciousness, she thought: 'So be it. I no longer care. Without Charles I have nothing.'

Then the darkness swallowed her up and she slept.

Chapter 26

The leaves were falling from the trees as Rachel moved through the marketplace looking for Charles. Where was he? He should be here; he was always here on a Wednesday. Then she remembered that he wouldn't be anywhere ever again, and she let out a muffled cry of despair. It had been three weeks now since Charles had gone (she still couldn't bring herself to say 'died') and the pain, if anything, seemed to be getting worse. She saw him everywhere she went, in the town, by the river, even in her room at night, but each time she got close to him, he disappeared. Was it Charles' spirit or just her imagination? Was she going mad?

She had returned to her job after a day of unconsciousness, mechanical and uncommunicative. The river of life flowed on, but it diverted around her, leaving her untouched. She barely spoke to anyone and when she did it seemed her stammer had returned, for she struggled to form the words she needed.

There had been no tears since the day of Charles' death. Everything was frozen up inside her and Rachel felt as if there was a heavy weight pressing down on her chest. At times it was hard to catch her breath, it was so oppressive.

Kitty had urged her to rest for longer, but Rachel could not stay in bed. For one thing her dreams tormented her. All she saw were images of ropes and blood, and she heard the drums roll again in her head.

Returning from the market Rachel found that she had, once

again, forgotten to buy the things they needed for dinner that night. This was happening frequently now, and she knew in her heart that she wasn't coping with the job.

'Kitty,' stumbled Rachel, 'I forgot, that is, I couldn't get the fish from the shop. It was closed, no busy, I mean. Can you go and fetch it please?'

'Yes ma'am,' said Kitty, concerned. 'Are you alright? You don't seem yourself.'

Rachel snapped at her. 'Don't be impertinent! I'm fine. Now go!'

Anger seemed to appear out of nowhere these days. Kitty's face clouded over.

'Yes Ma'am, sorry,' she replied and sped off. Rachel cursed herself for upsetting the well-meaning maid and made a silent vow to apologise later. When Kitty returned Rachel attempted to do just that, but she stuttered awkwardly.

'Kitty, I, that is, I know you mean well but I, well, I'm fine, really. Thank you.'

'Yes Ma'am,' said Kitty, but Rachel could see that something had been damaged. The kindly maid's hurt feelings would take time to heal. The younger woman left the room rapidly and Rachel stayed there feeling sad. Kitty had always looked out for her and now she had offended her. If only she could explain.

Time went on and more mistakes were made. Rachel was confused and forgetful in her work, leading to errors in the accounts, badly planned menus and lost laundry. Kitty only spoke when she had to these days and Polly was her usual grumpy self. The dreams of Charles were getting more frequent. It felt like he was trying to speak to her, but she could never quite work out what he was saying. He seemed so far away. In an attempt to get closer to him Rachel decided that she must visit his grave. If she could see his final resting place and lay some flowers, maybe it would give her some peace. Upon asking at Norman Cross for the whereabouts of the tomb, however, she was shocked to hear the guard laugh.

'Sorry, Miss, there ain't no grave. He's gone to the surgeon to be anatomised – cut up, if you know what I mean! Helps them young physicians if they got something to practice on. They were never gonna let 'im have a monument, anyway. Not a bad 'un like 'im!'

Rachel let out a cry of horror and rushed off, flinging the flowers away. Her poor Charles couldn't even be left alone in death. What a terrible thing.

The next morning after some dreadful nightmares, Rachel was called up to see the master of the house.

'Mrs Alderman,' the Reverend said, 'it seems you are having some problems at work. From what I hear we have run out of clean sheets again and the butcher's bill has still not been settled. What is going on? This is not like you,' he added, more kindly.

'Sir, I am doing my best, but I, well that is, I ….' Rachel stopped. How could she tell him the reasons when she barely understood herself?

'Can I help at all?' the Reverend asked.

'No Sir,' she muttered. 'No-one can.'

'Perhaps this job is too much for you now?' he said. 'Maybe it is time to make a change.'

'No!' she cried anxiously. 'Please Sir, this job is all I have. I will try harder, honestly.'

'Well alright, however please do so soon, otherwise I will have no alternative except to get someone else in. I'm sorry. I don't want to, you understand, but my household needs to be run smoothly and efficiently.'

'Yes Sir,' mumbled Rachel and went back to her room to consider what he had said. For the first time in many weeks her tears fell, and she couldn't stifle them any longer. Once she started, she couldn't stop for a long time. Everything came back to her – Charles, Rose, her sister Mary, her family. All lost to her, and now there was her job, where she was barely clinging on. The outpouring of sorrow brought her relief at last, and a clarity she hadn't had since September. Lying on her bed, exhausted by emotion she suddenly heard Charles' voice. Was it in her head? She sat up but he wasn't there, yet she could hear him clearly now.

'My darling, cherie, calm yourself. You must carry on.'

'I can't,' she cried, 'I need you so much.'

'I am here, all around you,' came the voice. 'I am always with you.'

'No', said Rachel. 'It's not enough. I want to be with you.'

'Patience cherie. We will be together again one day. In the meantime, you are stronger than you know. You can do this.' The voice faded away, leaving Rachel feeling bereft again.

'Charles don't go. Please!'

All was silent, except for the lonely wind howling outside.

The release of emotion had done Rachel good, and drying her eyes, she went back to work, determined to put things right. In the next few days, the finances were straightened up, bills paid, meals and laundry sorted, and the household was back on an even keel again. Even Kitty and Polly were happier, nevertheless Rachel felt no better. Her mind now was calm and clear, but there was still a desperate ache inside, a longing for her loved one. It was a void that she could never fill.

One rainy night Rachel dreamt of Charles again. This time she was able to see and hear him clearly. He looked as she had first seen him, healthy and handsome, dark hair in a ponytail and a charming smile. In her dream they walked by the river again, talking and laughing. Then Charles told her:

'I must go, now, my love, and soon I fear I will not be able to visit you again. My time here is nearly done.'

'No!' Rachel exclaimed. 'Let me come with you, Charles. I want to be with you, wherever that may be.'

'My darling, you must stay and live on.'

'No Charles, my love, we dreamed of being together for always. I know now what I must do. I need to join you.'

'Do not say that' Charles told her, 'I cannot bear to think of it.'

Rachel insisted. 'It's the only way. Then we can be together in eternity. I always said I would follow you anywhere and if it is to the afterlife, then so be it. My mind is quite made up, my love. You cannot stop me.'

'If you are certain, cherie, then I will be overjoyed to have you with me. We can be together forever. But I fear I have caused you so much distress.'

'Charles my love, you saved me from a life of loneliness and boredom. There is nothing without you, nothing.'

The figure of Charles came towards her, his arms outstretched.

'Then join me, my love. I am all yours.'

The vision ended and Rachel awoke, sure now of what she had to do. She locked the door and dressed quietly in the beautiful dress she had worn to the dance. The outfit brought back so many happy memories. Thinking for a few moments, she rearranged the room, moving the bedstead slightly. Then she removed her garter, tied it to the frame above her, and carefully positioned a chair. This action made her tremble for a minute, but she was determined now. Sitting on the bed for a while she took in the enormity of what she was doing and questioned herself in a deliberate manner. 'Is this what you really want?' Yes, was the answer, decidedly yes! 'Do you know what this means?' Again, yes! She reflected on her life as a whole. It only seemed to have started when she met Charles. Before that, she had just been waiting. Now he was waiting for her.

As she stood on the chair, the garter fastened loosely around her neck, she saw Charles' image before her, coming closer and closer.

'My love,' he said smiling, 'my eternal love. Come to me now.'

He reached out towards her and at last she was able to grasp his hands. A thrill of joy ran through her, and she felt the very air surge with love. Then, laughing in sheer happiness at their reunion, she jumped.

THE END

Authors note

Rachel Alderman was the sister of my 4 times great grandfather Henry. I am indebted to the wonderful Alderman one name study for the information that inspired this novel. The first document of interest was Rachel Alderman's will, dated October 1800, where she describes herself as: '*sick and weak in body, but of sound mind and memory.*'

Her estate was to be divided between her sister Elizabeth White and the children of her other sister, the late Mary Baker, as well as her brothers, John and Henry. Obviously, this illness whatever it was, did not prove to be her end for I found another later document which set me to much pondering.

To quote from '*The Alderman One-name project*':

'An entry under **deaths** in the '*Gentleman's Magazine of 27th November 1808*' records:'

"*Rachel Alderman, housekeeper to Rev Mr Tutte, one of the prebendaries of Peterborough Cathedral. She was found dead in her room, suspended by her garters from the bedpost.*"

These two records made me long to know more. For this reason, I started to research Peterborough in the 1800s to see if I could shed any light on Rachel's tragic demise. I was then surprised to find out about an institution I had never previously known existed: Norman Cross Prison camp – the first prisoner of war camp in Britain. This opened just outside Peterborough in 1797, closed in 1814 and was built to take prisoners from the

Napoleonic wars. My major source here was Paul Chamberlain's excellent book '*The Napoleonic Prison of Norman Cross*' which was invaluable to me. Reading this I discovered that many prisoners were given parole and allowed out into the city, where romantic entanglements with the local population often developed! When I searched further into the year 1808 (the year of Rachel's suicide), I found a record of the only prisoner to be publicly hung at the camp, Charles Le Boucher, taking place only about 6 weeks before Rachel's death. He had been convicted at the Quarter Assizes in Huntingdon, of '*cutting and wounding*' a warden, Alexander Halliday, whilst trying to escape. The coincidence was too good to miss. After all, why would a 40-year-old housekeeper to a vicar suddenly hang herself?

To the two tragic individuals I can only apologise for (possibly) taking their names in vain, but authors have to get their inspiration from somewhere and this was mine. Whatever the circumstances, I hope their souls will rest in peace.

References

The Alderman One-name Project by Bob Alderman in collaboration with Neil Alderman and Mari Alderman, independently published 2006.

Early Alderman Wills in Northamptonshire (1522 – 1858), collected transcribed and edited by Bob Alderman, Mari Alderman and Neil Alderman, independently published 2008.

The Napoleonic Prison of Norman Cross   The Lost Town of Huntingdonshire by Paul Chamberlain, published by the History Press, 2018.

Time Team, Channel 4, excavation and TV show, July 2009.

Title inspired by the song 'The King of the Coiners' by Steve Tilston on his excellent folk album Ziggurat, released 2008 on Hubris Records. If you like singer/songwriters, please check him out.

Websites

https://www.wessexarch.co.uk/our-work/norman-crosscamp-cambridgeshire

https://www.stilton.org/about-stilton/history/norman-cross/#gsc.tab=0

https://en.wikipedia.org/wiki/Norman_Cross_Prison

https://peterborougharchaeology.org/norman-cross-prison

https://www.thehistorypress.co.uk/articles/the-prison-ofnorman-cross-the-lost-town-of-huntingdonshire

Milton Keynes UK
Ingram Content Group UK Ltd.
UKHW040617171123
432742UK00004B/77